"THE STEEL BREAKFAST ERA is a feverishly bizarre journey through a world where flesh has taken on the quality of living poetry. Written in a first-person present-tense immediacy that gives you no time to question the strange events as they unfold, cmIII's style describes technology-as-magic in a straight-forward manner that hypnotizes as it informs. How he manages to infuse even the most grotesque imagery of twisted and broken limbs with a strangely erotic charge is something to be admired. Trippy in the extreme, compellingly told and resolutely modern in the storytelling, this is a book well worth owning if you want to keep an eye on the future of the genre."

- Scooter McCrae, writer/director of
  Shatter Dead and *Sixteen Tongues*.

ALSO BY
CARLTON MELLICK III
(in order of publication)

Satan Burger

Electric Jesus Corpse

Sunset with a Beard

Razor Wire Pubic Hair

Teeth and Tongue Landscape

The
Steel Breakfast Era

by

Carlton Mellick III

ERASERHEAD PRESS

Eraserhead Press
205 NE Bryant
Portland, OR 97211

email: publisher@eraserheadpress.com
website: www.eraserheadpress.com

ISBN 0-9729598-7-4

AUTHOR'S NOTE

I really like that Andy Warhol version of Frankenstein. There's something appealing about the distortion of a very well-known classic tale into something profane and tasteless. So I figured it would be fun to rip off Andy Warhol ripping off Frankenstein . . . But I changed my mind at the last minute and figured it was a stupid idea and decided to make it more like Re-animator than Frankenstein . . . But I realized that too was a stupid idea because there are more Lovecraft-inspired stories than the world knows what to do with. So I just wanted to write a book about a guy who makes a woman out of dead woman parts and this stitched-together woman turns out to be more than he can handle . . . But that too seems like a story that has been done a million times. Remember Frankenhooker? So I just decided not to think about it so much and write the stupid book. That's how I usually do it.

There are many varieties of themes in the subtext of my books that can be totally ignored without ruining the enjoyment of the stories (kind of like Frankenstein), but one theme I'd like to mention is the importance of art. I am a firm believer that the only purpose a human being can have on this planet is to create art. But I also believe that people create art every day without even knowing it. Sure there are writers, painters, musicians, actors, dancers, singers, cooks, fashion designers, animal breeders, taxidermists, but there are a lot of others out there besides the obvious. For example, a fat guy on the bus eating a meatball sandwich, he is creating art just by being himself. Or how about that guy who played *Kubiac* from Parker Lewis Can't Lose? Just his existence alone is sheer genius. He doesn't even have to do anything.

(By the way, a giant mutated toilet elf is more profoundly artistic than any Stephen Spielberg movie ever made. The bible says so.)

So my point: art is everywhere (except in Stephen Spielberg films). It surrounds us, drives us, and sometimes destroys us.

This book examines the more destructive kind of art. Art at its most violent. But the characters within are not always the artists. Sometimes they are the canvases, the brushes, the paint.

I've always had a fascination with becoming a work of art. A flesh painting. If my skin was like clay I would mold it into something else. Maybe I'd give myself some spikes or scales or twisty insect patterns. But having clay-skin is something that doesn't exist, not even in Star Trek.

The only thing we have in this society to modify our flesh into artwork is tattooing. Which, in my opinion, should be the highest respected artform of them all.

I have a bunch of self-designed tattoos, and one self-inflicted tattoo. I get one for every book I write. Otherwise I would just spend all my money on tattoos. I always wanted to have a tattoo of my face on my face or a tattoo of hair instead of hair. I don't really like having real hair or a face anyway.

I have included a bunch of photocopies of pictures of tattoos done by Pooch of alteredstate.net within this book. I normally illustrate or have someone illustrate my books but this time instead of regular drawings I decided to go with something different and more related to the flesh-art subplot. I think it turned out pretty dudical.

There's still nothing funnier than the term *dudical*.

Time for soup.

-- Carlton Mellick III, 12/10/03 7:45 am

This book is dedicated to Kathy Acker's tattooist

"When you sleep, you don't control your dream. I like to dive into a dream world that I've made, a world I chose and that I have complete control over."

- David Lynch

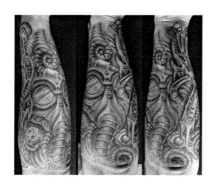

PART ONE
Electric Dead World

NUMBER ONE

"My mind falling out the back of my skull and creeping the drain . . ."

I wake to metal tik-worms sewing in and out of my skin. Inside of a bathtub filmed with hard meat.

Letting the tik-worms —-> thin thin silver maggots piercing into me, bone needles that seem electrical —-> crawl my legs for some intimate pain moments, just long enough for my senses to spark into life and organize.

They are deep down in me —-> in the red-white places where nerves and tendons form weaveworlds, molesting/eating my insides —---> digesting my flesh and then excreting it as metal. They hollow out the marrow and build little cities inside of me with their steel feces.

They have the ability to take control of my muscles:

something/someone opens my mouth and alien tin-noises issue from my throat. Sounds like hard rain hammering against sheets of aluminum. I close my mouth and the red-orange noise fades to a hum in the back of my head.

When I open it again, they return.

Nuzzling my way out of the bathtub . . .

I go dizzy. Hammering-rain noises streaming out of my mouth as I stand. Head heavy, and the tik-worms in my feet make it wobble hard to balance.

I pass two lovers on the floor near the toilet. They have been living here for weeks now —-> the metal worms have taken over their bodies and molded them together into one being, woven together with metal strands —-> lips welded to purple lips, brain melting into brain cunt becoming one with the penis.

A rotten pile of lovers, sitting together and twitching for movement . . .

My hands pull me over twiggy toes to the plastic sink.

The brown light makes everything look hairy ——> I notice a furry book full of fuzzy words over in the corner there and three wooly golf balls that must have been made out of a dead animal ——> as I dunk my hand into soupy black water, fingernailing sharp sink-things.

The corpse-like lovers begin to twitch again, licking each other and fighting the parasites their new metal parts. The female rolls her half-steel eyeball to me reflecting my image showing me what she can do with her breasts.

I pull a saw out of the black water. It is muddy with diseased blood. I clean it the best I can in the murk liquid, but it still looks coated in muck and disease.

Falling back on the toilet seat. I bring the saw's blade to my left foot

My eyes divert . . .

No, I change my mind. I want to watch. My feet must be removed properly.

Eyes back on target ——>

The saw slides through the flesh like dough, the tik-worms have made the flesh like clay. Rain-on-metal sounds vibrate inside my neck when I separate my feet from my legs. And after they slip off the bone and splatter onto the concrete floor, the alien sounds fade away.

No blood. As if they were artificial.

Inside of my discarded feet, I can see the metal pathways the worms had formed in me.

Several worms abandon the feet and wasp-squirm towards my open ankle. I push them back with the saw, a rough teeth-scraping noise, which doesn't move them as much as cut them into pieces.

The woman's eyeball continues to gawk, to wander up and down my body. I brush my severed feet into the tub like dirty clothes and crawl across the bathroom floor.

Inside a cabinet: a collection of heads from plastic baby-sized dolls. I decide to use two doll heads for feet, one with curly brown hair and green eyes and another with black-painted hair/eyes/skin, twisting them onto the ends of my legs.

Standing . . . awkward balance, holding myself with the tips of my fingers against the wall.

"The ship hasn't arrived yet," I tell the lovers, just in case they can still hear.

Clunk-clunking on the plastic doll heads . . .

The exit to the bathroom is coated in black mold.

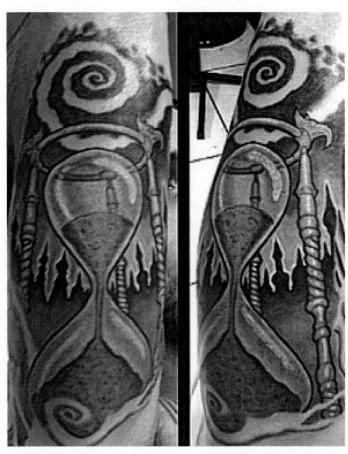

NUMBER TWO

"Slices of flesh scattered across the sticky asphalt . . ."

Out of the bathroom, clunk-stepping, the sun shining through the boarded windows in violent stripes.

My baby doll heads are filling with white leg fluid. I can feel the heads getting tighter around my ankles.

I go to the window to bathe in the brown-orange sun. Glance down at the hordes below —-> "Everywhere," examining the creeping ones, many stories down, in the ruins.

Their screams echo up the walls, pin-circling, screams that grow louder the farther they travel.

"Anta pay, anta pay." A tiny voice from behind.

Turning to see one of the children playing with a toy truck in the corner . . .

A little boy with no clothes. Tik-worms have stapled his hands to the toy, meat growing over the plastic —-> and parts of the truck have been molded into the child, extending up his arm, cutting into his brain.

"Anta pay, pacamo."

I can't tell if the child is saying real words or just disorder-mumblings. Maybe his parents never bothered to teach him language.

My doll head feet click-clunk up some stairs to the roof.

Outside:

A brown/orange blob that was once the sun. A rotten broken egg yolk. Its rays change my skin color into calico shades.

The distance:

A forest of platforms containing gardens and groves. The sun produces new types of crops —-> beetle-shaped nuts and human head fruits, vegetation resembling snakes, crabs, and insecty things. Melty black flowers that we cook in large vats for an earwig-flavored soup. All of this food is pungent and barely edible, probably toxic, but it is what keeps us alive. And I guess we are supposed to want to stay alive.

Sitting on the edge of the building to rest my legs, doll head feet dangling off into the sky . . .

Miles below, dead people are gathering and moaning. Their voices are louder than my thoughts. Tik-worms plague their flesh, turning most of their meat into metal. They are full of wires and plates and spikes.

Steel warrior zombies.

The doll heads fall from my feet. Their curly hair twisting in the wind.

This exposes a soft plumpness where the doll heads used to be. My feet have returned, swelled up from the legs, ballooned. The new feet are a texture like clay and have taken the shape of the mold that surrounded them.

So now my feet are in the shape of doll heads, staring up at me from the landscape.

NUMBER THREE

"Dinnertime in rancid spaces . . ."

am downstairs now, alone, in the dining area. It is a mess of dead
smells and hissing cockroaches and stuffed animals. A toy train circles
the table and makes electric choo-choo sounds.

Discarded limbs in a corner . . .

Water drips from the ceiling, so I stand open-mouthed to catch
the droplets, balancing on my new feet.

"Is it time to eat now?" asks an elderly gentlemen in red tights,
appearing from the doorway behind me.

The tables are missing plates of food. They are covered in toys
and stuffed animals. Mannequins and large dolls are in the seats where
people should be sitting.

I glance to the old man —-> a gritty-toothed fellow with a ribbon taped to his skull for hair.

"I don't know," I tell him.

They called us over the intercom to come down here for dinner,
but we are all alone. Only silence is here. It is loud with color, but quiet
of the screams of hungry people.

"Jesus loves you," says the old man, strapping a pink bra across
his chest.

"Maybe we should get our own food," I tell him and the old
man sits down and waits for me to serve him.

"Let's talk about something," says the old man.

"I don't talk."

And I walk upstairs, away from him, towards anywhere else.

NUMBER FOUR

"Balloons and dolls and grass skirts and blue carpeting disguised as the ocean . . ."

The Hawaiian Dance is supposed to be today, right now, where we all gather in one room and make believe we are in a better place. With some of us singing and some of us dancing. But down in the dance hall I am alone.

There is a painting of a beach and palm trees on all four walls to help us pretend we are in paradise. My face leaks yellow water as I stare at it, sitting down to drink punch and lighter fluid.

"Will you dance with me?" I ask a hula dancer in the painting in the background.

She says nothing. She is just a painting. The smile on her face is not a real smile.

Across the room ——> I notice some dancers have joined me in the distance. A man dancing with a woman and a woman dancing by herself. There is no music. I approach the lone woman to maybe dance with her . . .

Stepping closer, getting them in focus ——> the dancers are almost all metal.

They are eyeballing me when I arrive to them, seeping a dirty green odor with their insides opened up like a gory diorama. And they make me sick. They make me want to run away. The lone woman probably ten years older than me ——> a deformed face eating itself inside-out. She is pregnant and the baby has a limb dangling out of a hole in her gut.

I pass them, avoid them. Out of the dance. Not in the mood to see the deformed ones anymore. I'd much rather be with photograph of people than any real people . . .

NUMBER FIVE

"A little girl with half a face, cut down between her eyes, so we can look at the way her brain works . . ."

"The rotten man doesn't like you anymore," says the little girl with half a face.

"Who's the rotten man?"

She just smiles at me and puts a lollipop into her half-mouth.

"Will you be my boyfriend?" says the little girl, fluid leaking out of her brain down her shoulder.

Curly teeth.

I start to walk away from her, but:

"Be my boyfriend or the rotten man won't like you anymore."

Turning to her —-> the half-brain pulsating in my direction.

"Take me to the dance," she says. "I don't want to dance alone."

"I'm an adult," I tell the little girl. "I won't be with a child."

The girl strips herself of her clothing to reveal half-developed adult features —-> flat-saggy mounds with large nipples, stripe of pubic hair and dried blood. But her size and face is of an eight-year-old.

"I'm not a child," she says. "Go to the dance with me, hold my hand."

I take steps back from her on my doll head feet.

The girl folds her eyebrow into her mouth and rips it off at me.

"I am a princess!" she demands, blood sprinkling from her forehead.

I approach her, try not to look directly into her. Grab hold of her neck, lean her head back and she smiles. Then I open up her half-mouth and step inside.

Taking the secret passage to my bedroom . . .

NUMBER SIX

"I am covered with dirt and sores . . ."

Inside my room, in baggy sleep-clothes, my room down in this fleshy cave pocket. Just enough room for a large furry bed and a cabinet with a shadeless lamp. The bed is cluttered with objects collected and brought here —-> a mickey mouse clock, a gold button, a penny glued to another penny, a dog sculpture made of plastic hotdogs, a knife with a bird skull handle which always cuts me when I lose it between the sheets.

I also have a stack of photographs, my greatest treasures, that I crave to be inside of. The pictures are of happy times —-> families, vacations, lovers, bright clean clothing, smiles, babies, kitty-cats, holidays, school portraits. I look at them slowly, one-by-one, examining deeply, my eyes so close my entire vision enwraps into the photography.

Inside of their perfect worlds . . .

I want to be with them/die with them.

I especially want to die.

There is a woman in one of the photos that I wish I could die with. I stare at her more than the backs of my eyelids. She is clean with radio-blue eyes and waxy fabrics, pale-peach skin and a pretty scar up her left arm. And a violet tattoo on the side of her neck. I want to crawl up next to her and die right there.

There is nothing in the world I want more.

NUMBER SEVEN

"The prickle-weed emotions overwhelming me . . ."

Wandering downstairs to the lobby. I need to be with somebody. I don't care who. Just any normal human being.

People are always in the lobby. I don't like those people, the warriors, but at least they're alive and tik-worm free.

Taking the spiral staircase down several flights in the smooth white tube of stairwell, blinding white as I rumble the steps down to the bottom.

Opening a door to an ocean of people: screams/moans echoing the lobby . . .

Some zombies have made it through the barricade and are running around with eyeballs hanging out of their heads, metal bones sticking out of rotten meat.

The guards down here have sealed up the entrance but a dozen or so living corpses are still inside. Soldiers and zombies chasing each other around the lobby in a terrifying yet comical dance. Turning the lobby into a grand ballroom where the dancers eat and kill each other.

An axe breaks through a half-metal skull.

I can hardly tell the difference between the living and dead, both dirty and crazed and rotten and killers.

The zombie with an axe sees me, struggling to pull his crooked weapon out of a melty head on the floor. Soil-blood smeared across the tiles.

"Help us!" The zombie screams at me.

The axe-wielder is not a zombie. He is a living man wearing dead human flesh clothes. Perhaps a disguise . . .

I look the other way. Then look back.

"Is the ship here yet?" I ask him.

"What?" the man screams, sliding in gritty blood and losing his grip on the axe.

"Is the ship—"

A couple of zombies with spiky arms jump on the soldier from behind and tackle him to the blood pool.

"My axe!" he shrieks at me, and a zombie bites into his shoulder.

The man grinds his teeth and makes a squirm-ugly face at me, which makes me giggle but I try not to let him see me laugh at him.

I point at the axe in the zombie's head.

He nods, screaming, "Get it, get it!"

Strips of his flesh are in zombie mouths and the man squeals profanities at them.

I leave the doorway of the stairwell and pull the axe from the zombie's head.

"Yes, yes!" screams the man. "Throw it!"

And I examine the axe on the sharp side ——> It is quite rugged with a twisty handle and curly patterns on the metal. It's strong but seems delicate and antique-like. I wish I had a weapon like this.

I run my finger down the edge of the blade. It doesn't cut my skin. It needs sharpening. The knife-sharpener in my room could help it become sharp again. I should go sharpen it . . .

The man breaks my concentration with a piercing cry as the zombies tear out his spine through the back of his neck, his head goes limp on his chest, strings of meat dripping out of him like coleslaw.

I forgot to give him the axe . . .

The zombies eat the soldier's brain.

I wave my arms around at them to get them to stop ——> a distraction or something I guess. But they do not stop.

Well, I should sharpen it up for him anyway. This is such a nice axe. I might keep it for him.

Leaving the lobby and ascending the stairs where battle sounds become muffles . . .

NUMBER EIGHT

"In a rancid coffee lounge on the second floor . . ."

A green-haired man. No, I think his hair is brown but the lighting makes it appear greenish, and I'm not sure if it is actually a man either, maybe a woman. A man/woman. It is constructing a human-sized doll out of pieces of dead people. I also can't tell if the doll being created is male or female.

Putting genders aside, I am intrigued by this person's craft. Everyone should have a craft these days, something to keep the mind occupied, something constructive. My hobby is collecting interesting things, like this axe. My eyes glaze over the axe . . .

To the man/woman: "Very good to see another hobbyist still alive!"

The man/woman's face is cross, curled up eyebrows and strange holes in his/her cheeks.

"So what are you crafting?" I ask —-> my head spinning up and down the axe. "Are you making a doll? Is that your hobby?"

"I am making my wife," he/she said with a raspy stern voice. "It is not a hobby. I just want a lover."

My fingers tighten around the axe, quivering closer to the man/woman. "Are you saying you plan on pretending this doll is a woman for marrying purposes?"

"No, this will be a real living woman when I'm done," says the man/woman.

I stare firmly at the half-made woman on the table. Yes, she *is* real woman.

"I want one," I tell him/her.

"Then make one," the person says, deep in concentration.

"I don't know how."

"Mr. Howl showed me. Go to him."

"The doctor? He's still alive?"

The man/woman stops her/his work to speak with me.

"You'll find him in the under chambers. But he only helps his close friends."

"Am I a close friend?"

"He doesn't have any friends."

My face shrivels confused.

"Well, he says he has a friend named *The Cod*, but I don't think he really exists. Nobody else has ever heard of him. Tell the doctor you're a friend of The Cod and he'll treat you like a brother."

"Thank you," I say and rub his/her future wife on the shoulder. "Thank you." The woman's skin is unusually smooth and raspberry-scented.

"She has no tik-worms?" I ask.

"Mr. Howl knows how to make them immune to tik-worms. Too bad he couldn't do the same for us . . ."

My hand cuddles the back of the woman's cold veiny neck. She is like a beautiful fish.

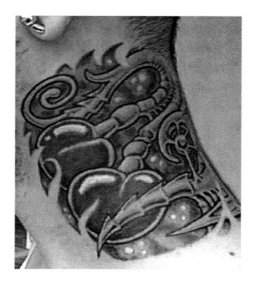

NUMBER NINE

"The Cod told me you could help me . . ."

The fuzzy old man continues to stare at me with a look of discomfort. His right hand has become metallic from the tik-worms living in his sleeve, his forearm woven into his chest like a sling.

"Mr. Howl . . ." I ask, tapping the axe handle on the counter. "I need someone to die with. A woman. I can't die alone, you know? I need a lover with me in the end."

"So you know The Cod?" Howl asks, going into excite-smiles. "How is he?"

My face ——> . . .

"Fine . . ." I tell him. "I saw him recently."

"Really?" Howl asks, eyes dazing, utterly amazed by these words. He acts as if I said the ship has come in or that I have some blueberries for him.

Finally, he continues. "Are you two good friends?

"Good friends?" My axe slips from my grip and thumps hard near my doll head feet.

I step on the axe but am too nervous to pick it up. So I pretend I never dropped it.

"Yeah, yeah, good friends," I say, fake-laugh voice. "I like the guy a lot."

"Me too," says Howl. "The Cod is a really great guy. Just a great guy."

He continues staring over my shoulder with a dumb smile on his face, sighing.

"Good times . . ." I tell him.

"Yes," says Howl. "Good times indeed."

Another silence. I don't like him. I don't like *indeed.*

"So what can I do for you?" asks Howl.

"I need a wife. The Cod says you can help me make one."

"Ahhh, yes," says Howl. "A new homemade wife is what every-one needs."

"I need one."

"Yes, they are so affectionate . . ."

NUMBER TEN

"The hall infested by large insects similar to blood-oranges with spider legs and snail eyes . . ."

Mr. Howl has given me a copy of the instructions on how to make a woman and a booklet on how to make a human soul. Plus all the chemicals and tools I'll need to create her. However, there are several ingredients I'll need to find. Most importantly, I'll need plenty of human flesh.

He told me I might be able to get help from Mr. Hometik, who is Mr. Howl's enemy. They were friends, maybe lovers, a long time ago. But one time Mr. Hometik said to Mr. Howl that The Cod was a disgraceful and worthless human being, and Mr. Howl will never forgive him for that.

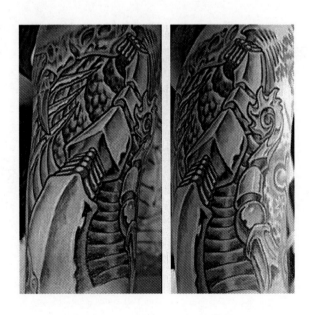

NUMBER ELEVEN

"Hello, Mr. Hometik . . ."

Knocking on a door coated in barbed wire, my knuckles bleeding, blood droplets on the cement floor.

No answer yet, but it has only been a second. I am very impatient.

I knock again.

Some skin peels back but the blood doesn't flow any faster. A few large blotches on the floor.

The door opens before I have to knock again. An older man with one large monocle for a right eye and an open hole with twisty metal maggots for a left eye.

"And you are?" asks the elderly gentleman with brown leather clothes.

"I am building my wife, and . . ."

"Ahh!" interrupts the man with a finger pointing upwards. "You are a creator of love! Come in, come in."

The old man hurries me inside and locks the barded wire door behind us. "I was about your age when I made my first wife."

He sits down in a pile of chair pieces, facing me. "She was not very well made. But being an unloved shriveled young man, I was happy to find any love at all. And though sewn together with eyes that were constantly bleeding, she was still better looking than any woman I pictured myself marrying. I wanted to be with her forever and ever."

"I want a woman to die with," I tell him.

"Good, they are utterly perfect for dying with. Are you in need of parts?"

"That's why I've come."

The man nods and tik-worms fall from his head. "Very good."

And he opens a milk carton on the floor revealing steps tha spiral into dark places. "You'll find them in here."

Taking steps down into the empty milk carton ——> sour smell creeping as the old man folds the carton behind me, enclosing me i darkness.

Alone.

My eyes blink two times.

A light explodes ahead. The old man lighting a torch, appear ing out of the shadows into foreground. Or is it not the same old man It seems like another person.

"Over here," the old man says, worms twitching out of his blac profile.

He pulls a couple buckets out of a wet hole. I step closer. The are filled with shifting female body parts, soggy and colorless.

"You can start molding these parts."

"Are they plastic? Rubber?"

"No, this is real flesh. They are pieces from the living dead The chemicals keep them from rotting. You build it into the woma you want and then give it a soul."

"It sounds difficult."

"Not really. I've made twenty-seven women in my lifetime. I'v never had any difficulties."

The body parts wiggle at me to put my lips on them. Squish sounds and I blink two times.

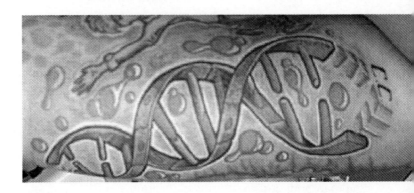

NUMBER TWELVE

"Carrying buckets of squishy female parts . . ."

The little old girl with half a head is naked in front of me again, commanding me to love her.

"You are too young," I say. "I've told you before."

The little girl with half a head says:

"Everyone says I'm too young, but I am a grown woman. I need love or I will die."

I smile. "I feel the same as you, but I have found a solution."

"What have you found?"

She stands there in her sick nudity, excited, awaiting my words. But my giggly facial expressions take control of me and I can't seem to get words out.

So instead of a reply I grab hold of her left nipple and twist it like a doorknob, opening her chest like a door. Her face dumbfounded when I slide into her torso, feet first, and close her chest/door behind me.

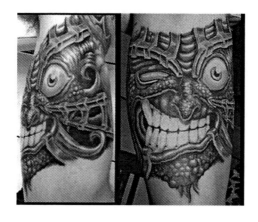

NUMBER THIRTEEN

"Somebody outside of my bedroom is being nailed to the ceiling . . ."

A gang of black hoods will do this to people on occasion. They will corner a person and then crucify them upside-down. But these men/women do not stop at three stakes. They use nail guns and fire miniature stakes into the victim until every limb is tight to the ceiling, so that the person will be crucified up there forever. Even after it comes back from the dead as a zombie.

At first, the black hoods only crucified people infested with tikworms, but now they do this to anyone they come across.

I am fondling through the body parts on my bed, trying to ignore the female shrieks outside the door. Blankets under my knees as I mold the flesh like clay to form smooth female skin.

"I need some good eyes," I tell the rotten black eyeball twisting in my fingers, examining me. "Eyes are the most important part."

The photo of the lovely angel-woman with glowing blue eyes is glued to the lamp so I can see her all the time. She is the woman I want to create.

The shrieking stops but the sound of nails thudding into the ceiling continues.

The hands I have for the woman are perfect. I lie here, stroking the thin female fingers that curl slowly around my wrist.

NUMBER FOURTEEN

"Alone for several days with only quivering female body parts to keep me company . . ."

The intercom called a meeting. I have come to it. To the room with many desks and very dim lighting. But I am the only one around. The room hasn't been used in at least a year. A chamber full of ghosts.

    Waiting . . .

    No one comes. My body rocking in the wooden squirmy corners, against webs and gritty old food ——> a corpse collecting dust in the corner . . .

    A few hours pass.

    My voice echoes softly in the butter-textured shadows.

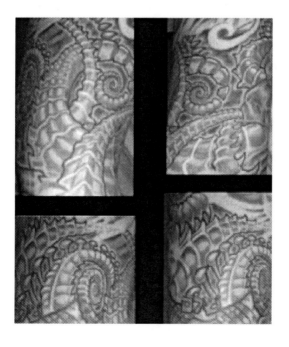

NUMBER FIFTEEN

"Doll head feet stained in blood, giving them red hair and freckles, blushing cheeks . . ."

Down in the lobby again ——> there are no people. Just the sounds of the living dead trying to break through the barricade. I take slow steps across the cold tile, doll head feet stumpling me.

Where are the guards?

None of them are here. People are always supposed to be down here watching the barricade or fighting the living dead. But their post has been abandoned.

I scurry through discarded body parts that clutter the floor. Walking on thick films of blood and rot. I don't want to use the rotten pieces to make my wife. Maybe if I cut the rotten spots off like mold on bread . . .

Picking up limbs and chunks of meat, examining, placing the fresher ones into my knapsack.

I still need a face.

Staring across the lobby, up the walls. None of the flesh here is worthy of my wife's face. Zombies are screaming at me through the barricade. I am now covered in blood and it makes them ravenous.

Into the barracks. A square tan room with blankets and couches for beds. It is also empty of people. And there aren't any body parts here at all.

When I enter, I slip. My doll head feet go out from under me and I land on my back. The floor makes an echoing pop sound when my skull hits.

My vision is blurry, facing the ceiling.

And some sharp pain quivers my body, starting at my fingers and ankles and then bolting into the back of my head.

When the blur clears, I am focused on the guards above me.

"There you are," I say to the corpses nailed to the ceiling.

Seven guards are here ——> five men, two women. Dead. Just hanging there, crucified. Blood raining out of them and onto the floor, onto my face, like their bodies are rain clouds. I hold out my hand to stop the blood from drizzling into my eyes. The floor has been painted red. And it is too slippery for my round feet to stand on, so I stay lying on my back watching the crucified soldiers rain themselves dry.

My eyes are still a little cloudy. The pain is like acid eating the backside of my head.

I gaze deeply at the guard directly above ——> a female.

Her black and red striped hair dripping down. Beautiful green eyes wide open, popping out of her face at me. Her arms are stretched out in the crucifixion position. Staring up at her as if she is about to wrap those arms around me, embrace my cold body.

I try getting myself to my feet. Sloppy. I have to wipe the blood pool out from under me so I can stand, leaving a clean yet sticky surface. Reaching up, my doll head feet wriggle. I grab onto her shoulders to balance, getting a good close-up view of her.

I can see all of her details now. Even her cute lip wrinkles, probably caused from smiling too much. I love her.

I've never seen her before. Was she always a guard? Was she hiding somewhere? Perhaps she is an unrotten zombie that got in. Doesn't matter, I guess. She is here. And she's better than I could hope for.

Look ——> I can't stop smiling at her. She is dead and mutilated but still I love her. Love is cute.

I get a grip under her chin and behind her neck. Then pull down. I have to use all of my weight. Once I lift my legs off the ground, I hear snapping sounds inside of her neck and sounds like stretching plastic.

My grip slips and I fall, but I get right back to it.

I twist her neck around. A bone tears through the side of her throat and I keep twisting, widening the wound, using the spinal bone to cut the skin. And then one more twist around, with a swish-crack,

the head pops off. Blood empties out of her neck onto me, but I let i
flow. I am busy looking into her face and smiling.

Then I kiss her deeply, wrapping an arm around the open spac
as if there is a body attached to the severed head.

Red rain drizzling down our foreheads . . .

NUMBER SIXTEEN

"In my bedroom, asleep, dreaming about fingers crawling through my hair . . ."

I am on my bed constructing the wife in a landscape of purple-black clouds and swirls of metal vegetation.

To make her soul, I can use any ingredients. The booklet says all objects have character and soul. If I dissolve certain objects into the fluid that acts as her blood-substitute, she will possess a soul. She will also have particles of soul leftover from the people who used to own the body parts that she will be assembled from. All of the particles will mix together to make one soul, one personality, one character.

In the preparation notes, the first thing I must do is give her a name. You must address the pieces you work with as she is being constructed, so it is best to address her by this given name.

I am very bad with naming things, but I guess anything will do. A name is not very important anyway.

I carve three letters into the left arm that will soon be hers.

The letters are: C Y N

They will have to do. I was going to write out C Y N T H I A, but I stopped at N for some reason. Perhaps in the back of my head I heard the soul of my future wife telling me to use Cyn instead of Cynthia.

I use these ingredients to make her soul:

1. A green candle.
2. A smiling plastic frog.
3. A red plaid shoe.
4. Some dried up rose petals.
5. A cute daddy long legs spider.

6. Two drops of red wine.
7. Three dashes of pumpkin spice.
8. A liquid faerie tattoo.
9. A sweet fruit similar to a cherry to make her soul smell like yummy candy.

I mold and sculpt the flesh into a woman, using the picture of my perfect angel as reference. Things are different, though. Instead of glowing icy blue eyes Cyn has emerald green eyes. And I can't get the hair to stay correctly on her head, so she is going to have to be bald. I also make her only about 5 feet tall, because I am running out of body parts.

The body parts start working before I put her all together. They rub against me, excited to come alive. And the arms start helping me construct the rest of her, knowing even better than the instructions how to make her body whole.

My dream fades after that, takes me into another place, into a nightmare of the living dead and metal tik-worms and being crucified to ceilings . . .

NUMBER SEVENTEEN

"Something warm, tight against me . . ."

I awake in darkness to a warm body against mine. It is a woman's. I can feel her breasts against my chest. This is not a dream.

Did I create a woman in my sleep or is she someone else?

My head still hurts and the darkness makes me dizzy.

I feel the buckets. They are still full of meat. She is someone else. She slithered into my room, sneaked into my bed.

Do I turn on the light and confront her?

My head doesn't want to move from the pillow. My body doesn't want to move from her body.

There is a chance this is not real, so I do not turn on the light. I lie here, holding the woman, feeling her breath against my neck. Consuming the moment and thinking about a piece of paper with sailboats and mustard on it.

PART TWO
Eaters of Love and Flesh

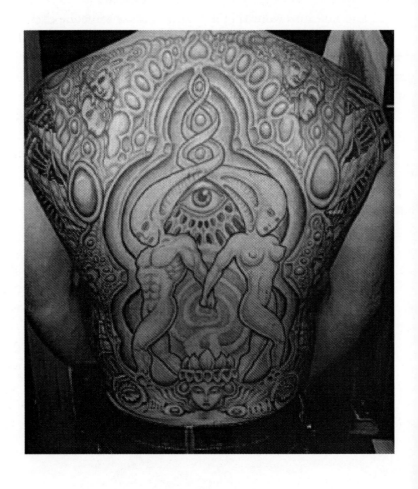

NUMBER ONE

"Kisses and sweet juices on my stomach and chest . . ."

She is real. The woman from last night is still here. My light on. Wide awake.

The girl is sitting naked on my bed —-> a patchwork of flesh tones and body parts. She has no hair and the back of her skull is jagged/pointy, like an eagle with flesh feathers. But her smile is lovely blue flowers. The lips of the soldier in the barracks, lip-wrinkles from smiling too much.

Even though I remember feeling the buckets full of flesh parts last night, they are empty right now. Clean like there were never any parts in there at all. It must have all been real. I must have created a wife last night. I can even see the letters on her left arm: C Y N.

"Cyn," I say.

The woman nods at me and smiles.

"You're very . . . very . . ." All words escape me.

"I want to explore!" the woman says in an angry tone.

My eyebrows curl. "What?"

The book said nothing about the woman being able to speak coherently or intelligently. They are supposed to be like pets. Like kitty-cats.

I am afraid of her.

"I'm bored of being in this room," she says. "Let's go walk around."

I laugh, shivering, almost cry. She is more real than I could have imagined. A real woman in front of me, in my room, my bed, naked with me, wanting to do things with me.

I am about to nod but . . . I notice my ugly feet.

"I'm not very good at walking," I tell her.

I show her my feet and she squints at them as if she has seen feet like mine before, like it is not uncommon for people to have doll head-shaped for feet . . .

"I'll fix you," she says.

She takes my bird skull knife from under the covers and cuts slices off of the doll heads —-> like carving clay or like peeling skin from an apple. I can feel it but there is no pain.

My eyes are glued to Cyn as she works, cat-elbowed with that knife. But —-> She puts a slice of my feet into her mouth and chews it. Then swallows.

I cringe at her.

"What are you . . ." I say, shaking my head.

She doesn't seem to have a problem with it, eating the pieces of meat she cuts off of me.

When she is finished carving, I see that my feet look like real feet again. The toes don't move very easily, but at least I can walk on them. Cyn stuffs the last of my feet scraps into her mouth and with a cheek-full of my meat she says, "All better."

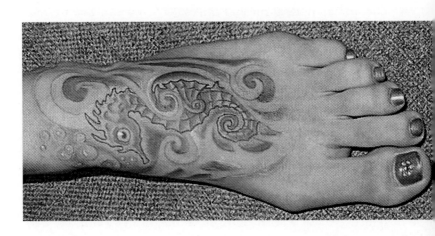

NUMBER TWO

"My feet mold-forming against the icy concrete floor, walking on them like normal feet only softer . . ."

Exploring the halls with Cyn. She is wearing a blanket for clothes, naked underneath and some of her chest and back is exposed.

Everywhere we go, there is the aroma of death. Rancid flesh littering the floor and sometimes a person woven into the wall overrun with tik-worms. These sights and smells do not bother her.

"I feel right at home," she says and her words make my head cock from side to side.

My eyes follow her movements —-> thighs and neck skin. She is utterly amazing. Even better than a real woman. Her patched together body makes her look as if she is covered in elegant tattoos. I am trembling in her vampiregoddess-like presence.

"Where is everyone?" she asks. "Are we the only people living here?"

Cyn is right. We haven't run into anyone today.

"There aren't many people left. A few dozen, maybe, and the majority of them are dying of tik-worms."

"I want to see some people."

"I'm not sure where to find them. They are mostly dying."

"Then let's look for them."

I agree. So we wander the halls for hours looking for a person. But we only find more human remains.

"This is horrible," she says. "None of these people are fresh."

"Yes," I tell her. "They have been rotting for weeks."

"Are you sure there are others alive?"

"They're probably all hiding."

I decide to take her to Mr. Hometik's room. He will still be alive. The tik-worms are not going to kill him for a couple more weeks, I'm sure. Plus I want to show him my new wife. He'll probably be amazed at the wonderful craftsmanship.

NUMBER THREE

"He's dead . . ."

Mr. Hometik's door has been torn open and his room ransacked. He is crucified to his ceiling. Droplets of fresh blood. He must have been murdered only moments ago.

"Dead, dead, dead." Cyn kicks at cans on the floor.

"Sorry . . ." I tell her.

"What put him on the ceiling like that?" she asks.

"There is a cult of crazies around. They want everyone dead."

"I hate them," she says.

"I've never seen them before."

"They must be the color green."

Cyn breaks a finger off of Mr. Hometik's left hand and puts it in her mouth, gnawing on it like candy.

"Let's try somewhere else," she says.

I nod, trying to ignore the knuckle dangling out of her lips.

And she breaks off another finger for later.

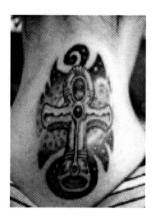

NUMBER FOUR

"Quivering pieces of skin, wire spiders dancing in the candle light . . ."

All day long, we search. But everyone is either nailed to a ceiling or completely overrun with tik-worms.

"I want people to be alive," says Cyn, rubbing her belly patches.

"The only people still alive are the ones who want us dead."

"This is not fun."

We go in the direction of the cafeteria.

"I don't want to go that way," says Cyn. "It's too green."

"It is the only place we haven't checked."

"But it is green. It must be where the killers live."

I pull her hand. "Come, we'll never find anyone by avoiding all the green rooms."

"I don't want to find people if they are killers."

Her patchwork flesh quivers under the meat-stained blanket.

NUMBER FIVE

"Steps like broken toes . . ."

In the room, which is slightly tinted green and where silver maggots live
in abundance over living corpses stapled to the walls ——> there is . . . a
man.

A living person . . .

"Is it someone else?" says Cyn.

I pinch her right thigh and wary-approach the figure.

The man is resting against a wall. We know he is not dead
because he is smoking a cigarette and his clothes are clean. So clean that
he is mirror-shiny, and our reflections are all over him.

"Is he a killer?" asks Cyn. "He might put you on the ceiling."

Closer to the man ——> he does not attack. He is busy smoking
and relaxing against the wall. He holds an umbrella-like hat and a weapon
that is a combination axe and boomerang. Several knife-spikes porcupine his arms and legs, and his boots are made of razors.

He is definitely a killer, but he does not attack.

When we arrive to him, he steps forward and examines us with
eyes like scalpels. There is no speed in his movements. Cat-creeping.
He reveals his teeth, teeth made of glass, and he begins to circle us like
prey.

"Are you a killer?" Cyn asks the man.

The man twists his head at her.

I notice his neck is thin and translucent, an icicle, nothing inside of it. I'm not sure how he can speak or eat or even smoke the
cigarette that he is smoking.

"I don't think he can speak," I tell my wife. "He has no vocal
chords."

Then he lunges at us, throws us to the ground ——> shiny weapon spiraling in the air.

NUMBER SIX

"War-screams and rumble blood storms, cut jugulars, tic-violence surrounding us, on top of us . . ."

We are being attacked by men with black hoods and nail guns, tikworm infested men with baggy skin and sewing machines for mouths.

They sweep through from all doorways of the room, battle-crying at us. Blood is getting in my eyes. Black robes billowing in shadow.

The man ——-> the one with the shiny clothes and glass teeth. He is also all around us. He fights the black hoods, slicing through them with his axe/boomerang, jumping and lunging like it is ballet.

"He is a killer of killers," Cyn cries.

Nails pierce into his chest and face, but he continues to slash apart the group of black hoods. A nail staples his hand to the wall, plastering him there, and before he can free himself a black hood amputates his arm with a boxed sawing device. But he continues to fight with one arm.

Then a nail pins his foot to the ground. No, several nails are in his foot. The black hoods back up, their sewing machine mouths rankering at us, and they shoot at him out of range from his winging arms.

He throws the axe at the crowd. It carves into them and returns. He throws it again, but he is getting weak. The nails are filling up his flesh and it is getting hard for him to move.

NUMBER SEVEN

"Run . . ."

We need to get out of here. The man with glass teeth is losing his battle with the black hooded ones and after he is killed we will be crucified to the ceiling.

I grab Cyn by the wrist and pull her up.

"Let's go . . ."

We run across the room, across the line of fire, and get drilled with dozens of flying nails. I feel them opening up the meat on my back as I collapse to the ground. Cyn underneath me. And I can't help myself. I can't move.

Lying here with blood leaking out of me ——-> and Cyn licking up my blood . . .

NUMBER EIGHT

"Dreaming of fish with long gooey tongues . . ."

Cyn wakes me with excited pushes. Her delicate scorpion-breath on my neck, warm naked body against me under the blanket.

I see a room filled with nails and corpses. Black hooded bodies in a pile. People are talking in languages I can't understand.

My head pulls itself out of dreamland.

There are two people dragging the black hooded corpses into a pile, making swirly beeping noises. One is female and has chains for hair, but I do not see all of her from the shadows. I can mostly see the other, who is a man/aquarium; his flesh is like glass with water and exotic fish inside. He has no insides other than the fish, no heart or muscle. His head is a human head, but his body is all aquarium.

I am nude under the blanket with Cyn. All of the nails have been taken out of me and the holes are starting to heal. Cyn's warmth is making all of the pain go away.

On the other side of the room is the man who was fighting with the black hoods. He is being put back together by a man with a red cape, who dances with his neck.

Four of them . . .

"Who are they?" I ask.

"I thought you knew," Cyn says.

As the strange people move the corpses of the black hoods, one of the bodies comes back to life, kicking and screaming.

The strange people make swirl-beeps at him, but he doesn't understand and just screams at them with his sewing machine mouth.

The man in the red cape turns around, neck-dancing —-> he is tall with crazy blond hair and has a small dresser instead of a chest and cabinet legs. He scurries to the black hooded man and rips off the black hood, revealing a messy distorted face. Then he opens one of the drawers on his chest to retrieve an electric cutting device. With this, the red-caped man removes the sewing machine from the crazed man's mouth, silver gook spewing onto the floor.

I get a good look at the crazy man without his black hood. He is bald and covered in scabs. I remember his face from somewhere. He is my brother or my father or someone really familiar I think. But I am not sure. Perhaps he was only my brother or father in a dream. I don't remember ever meeting him or talking to him. Yet I feel that I know him . . .

He yells at the strange people with a waspy voice, "Get away, get away, get away."

The woman makes swirl-beep noises to the man/aquarium and the red-caped man. They open up their necks to fidget with small gadgets that look like the insides of clocks.

"Is your translator working?" the woman asks the red-caped man.

"Yes, I believe so," he replies.

"Akira?" she asks the aquarium man, who nods at her.

The crazed person is still kicking and screaming, still familiar to me in a way that twitches nerves under my eyelids.

"We don't want to make you like the others," the woman tells the crazed man. "We are here to save you from the dead ones."

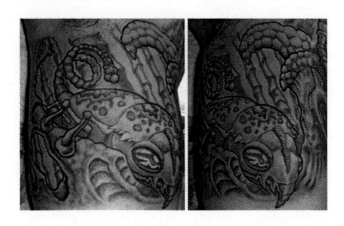

NUMBER NINE

"My eyes light up at her words, hugging Cyn against me and trying not to smile . . ."

"The ship has arrived?" I ask the woman. "Hasn't it?"

Her head turns to me without moving her body, a clicking noise when it moves. Then it turns all the way around to question the red-caped man.

"They are also survivors," the red-caped man says. "But they are not violent. Tsuko rescued them."

The woman's head spins around her neck until it is facing forward and she approaches us.

"We are a small army sent to save you from the living dead who plague your country," says the woman. "I am Miki, communications and science officer of our unit."

She points to the red-caped man, "This is Ran, our doctor," and to the man/aquarium, "This is Akira, our scout," and then to the man with the shiny clothes and glass teeth, "And that is our fighter, Tsuko, who saved you from those who wanted you dead."

I don't know what to say to her. The woman, Miki, has gleaming dark eyes that paralyze me, make me want to keep looking into them and forget about the rest of the world.

"The commander of our unit, Ryo, is downstairs. He will be back shortly and we can get you out of here."

"You're not at all green," Cyn tells them.

The woman smiles at Cyn.

"You are not like the others," Miki says about Cyn.

"She is not human," I tell her.

"He made me out of leftover body parts," Cyn says.

The doctor raises an eyebrow, "Interesting . . ."

"We also use this technology," says the woman.

The fighter, Tsuko, is back together again and stands up shiny-skinned. He ties the prisoner with a squishy rope and puts him out of their way, a few yards from us.

"He won't try to hurt you again," Miki says. "I can see into his mind. He is also a victim like yourselves."

"When will you take us away from here?" I ask.

"Soon. Just sit tight."

Over the woman's shoulder we see Tsuko and the aquarium man hooking long plastic tubes into the dead bodies, draining their blood into metal ball-shaped containers. Next to them, the doctor cuts large pieces of meat from the draining bodies, collecting the flesh chunks and placing them into the drawers on his chest and legs. I can see inside his chest when he opens the drawers. And like the aquarium man, he has no human insides, no internal organs. Just a hollow shell.

"What are they doing?" I ask the woman.

She looks back at the men, pausing, then stares at me with her snake-black eyes.

"Fresh meat and blood is very precious to us," she says. "Our kind cannot survive without it."

I stare back at her, not able to respond while deep in her eyes.

When I wake from the trance, I turn to Cyn —-> she is smiling at me with blood smeared on her mouth, a large chunk of meat in her palms. The doctor is throwing meat scraps to her like she's a begging dog. She sits there, smiling at him and then to me and then to him, wagging her naked butt like a tail.

NUMBER TEN

"There's something wrong with the earwig people living behind the wall . . ."

I do not know if my wife is in love with me. I created her to be in love with me, but she only seems to love me when I feed her trimmings of my feet after they grow shaggy. She smiles at me a lot and is always really close. It's like she's known me forever. But I don't know anything about her. She is mystery. Mystery scares me.

I don't know if I'm in love with her either . . .

The man with the sores keeps staring at us. He doesn't look very tough without his black hood on, but I still don't like the way he's staring at us.

The four machine-like rescuers don't do anything when they see him bug-eyed at us. They are busy talking into a telecom to their commander. "Are you there? Are you there?" they keep saying.

"Stop staring at us," I yell at the black hood.

The man shrieks and covers his face.

He begins to cry.

Cyn sees him crying and makes a sad face at me. She tries to comfort him.

"What's your name?" she asks, her cheeks turning red.

"Ronald," says the man, in whimpers.

"Why did you try to kill us?" Cyn asks.

"Don't talk to him," I whisper to Cyn. "He's crazy."

Cyn grinds her nails into my inner thigh, just next to my crotch, mad for the interruption.

"You deserve to die," cries the man.

I can hear Cyn licking her lips while she talks to him, getting excited by his smells.

Her eyebrows ask, "Why?"

"Everyone deserves to die. Men are death machines. They are created to cause death or become dead."

"Then why didn't you kill yourself?" I tell the man.

He widens his eyes at me, red-angry.

He cries to me, "Do you think I want to be a death machine? Do you think it's easy being surrounded by all this death and murder? Our world is pure chaos. It drives you to killing or to being killed."

I close my eyes. Cyn is clawing at my feet, drooling at the man. She can't hear a word he's saying anymore.

"Do you think I chose to be this way?" cries the man. "Don't you understand? I am a victim. I am the one who is compelled to steal life from doomed innocents. Don't you have any compassion?"

She licks the back of my neck, glaring at the man through the corners of her vision.

NUMBER ELEVEN

"Miki is picking and eating metal tik-worms out of Ronald, he is bound and gagged, unable to struggle against her slithering fingers . . ."

"There are things people never get to see or feel," I explain to Cyn.

"Are they ugly things?" Cyn asks. "Green things?"

"No, they are usually good things that we miss. Blue and purple things. You will miss even more than I have missed. And I have seen mostly ugly things."

"I'd rather be blind than see ugly things."

"Everything looks nice when I'm with you."

I smile and she smiles back.

"Let me eat your feet-shavings," she tells me.

"What?"

"Cheer me up. I want to eat pieces of you."

"My feet are not shaggy now. You just shaved the extra meat an hour ago."

"But I have this terrible craving that won't let go."

She rubs her patchwork breasts against my shoulder. "Let me have some fresh meat."

"Fresh meat?"

"Just a little from your arm or shoulder."

"I don't like pain."

"If you love me the pain won't matter."

"But . . . I don't even know if you love me."

"You created me. I have no choice but to love you."

"I need you to love me freely. Not because you think you have to. I don't want you to say you love me unless you truly do."

"I think I mean it."

"If you loved me you wouldn't want to hurt me."

"You're the one hurting me. I'm dying of hunger and you won't let me eat pieces of you."

"We can find other meat for you."

"But I want yours. You're the one I love."

She moves away from me, pouting. Crossing her arms around her belly.

"I'm sorry."

"I'll fuck you if you give me some of your meat."

"You're my wife. We don't fuck, we make love."

"Let's make love, then."

"No, let's go back to sleep."

"No, let's make love. Now."

She crawls on top of me and wraps her lips around my neck, rubs her crotch against my thigh. She doesn't have any pubic hair, so I can feel the labia spreading against my knee. I don't like hair very much anyway. She is bald and smooth. She has eyebrows, though. Only eyebrows and lashes.

"I'll bite into you just before you orgasm," Cyn tells me. "That's when pain feels really good."

NUMBER TWELVE

"Blood crusts over the holes in my back, the bite on my shoulder, the crack in my head . . ."

"What? What?" Miki says to her communication device, the voice on the other end is all static and screech-noises to me. "Stay there. We come there to you. Stay. No. Do nothing. Stay."

She clicks the communicator off and speaks to the doctor.

"Ryo is in trouble," she says. "The dead have flooded the first three floors. He is without escape."

"How long will he last in his current position?"

"He says several days, but I believe less time."

"We must get him out of there."

"He says to get the survivors to the ship first. And he says to hurry. The dead can smell the blood in this room."

"Okay, we go now," says the doctor. "Tsuko," waking the fighter from meditation, "get ready. We go now."

Tsuko twists into battle stance, his arms and legs folding out like butterfly knives. He opens his crotch armor and a hand-shaped mechanical penis emerges, stretching its fingers. The little cock-hand draws a thin razor-sword from Tsuko's thigh and swings it at the doctor for a salute.

The doctor opens a drawer on his chest and pulls out a small weapon device, similar to the combination of a crossbow and a catapult. He loads it with steel-spiked balls. The others draw their weapons as well: Miki removes her left arm and folds it open and around until it transforms into two axe-shaped weapons. She throws one to the aquarium/man (Akira) who jumps up to catch it, disturbing the fish inside of him.

"What about us?" I ask. "We need weapons too. I have a knife and a super fancy axe in my room."

"We can't let you fight in your current state," Miki says. "We will protect you."

"But what if you die? We must defend ourselves."

"If the dead defeat us they will surely defeat you. Your only defense is to flee."

I look at my deformed clay feet and begin to panic.

NUMBER THIRTEEN

"Stepping through a moist-grey hallway, its walls made of bodies sewn together with metal wires . . ."

"They don't even look human anymore," Cyn says to the walls.

Even the mechanical people are amazed by what the tik-worms have done to the bodies. Even me.

"This was not here when we entered," says the doctor.

"I've never seen this here before, either," I tell them.

"It is artwork," Miki says.

Artwork? I examine the walls. The flesh has been mutated into curvy patterns.

"I doubt the worms had creative intentions," the doctor says.

"You just refuse to believe," Miki says. "Everyone knows that all their intentions are creative intentions."

"That has never been proven," the doctor replies.

"What are you talking about?" I ask. "You need intelligence to create art."

"The tik-worms have intelligence," Ran says. "They have sort of a collective mind, we believe. Or perhaps the intelligence is artificial. We are not sure."

"The tik-worms are clever little parasites," Miki says with almost a smile. "They have the power to manipulate flesh, control it, turn it into whatever they want."

"And they control the zombies, don't they?" I ask, squeezing my fists. "I always figured they were the reason the dead came back to life."

"Exactly," the doctor says.

"It has not been proven," Miki tells the doctor.

She turns to me. "The new theory is that the tik-worms are not the cause for the dead's hostility. We believe the only purpose of the tik-worm is to create intricate sculptures using living flesh as its medium. First, they try to spread throughout a living body. They reform the legs and arms until the animal is immobilized. Then the worms kill the brain. They will keep the flesh alive by feeding it the proper nutrients, but the brain will be dead."

I notice I have been slowing the group down a little for conversation. Ran grabs me with a hook of fingers and quickens me to his pace.

He tells me, "That is all true, but what is under debate is what the worms do with the flesh once it overcomes a victim. The leaders of our country agree that the tik-worms are an alien species who want to conquer our world. They use the flesh of some of their victims to form cities which are more like a beehive or ant colony. But many of their victims stay in human form. They are used as warriors for the tik-worm collective, attacking surviving humans to make it easier for the worms to overcome its victims."

Miki peeks her head over my shoulder. "But the new theory is that the flesh-eating dead were not created on purpose by the tik-worms. We believe that sometimes the tik-worms fail to kill the human brain fully. Some of it still lives and can overpower the worms. They have been reduced to crazed half-dead barbarians who are driven only by deranged primal instincts. All they can do is kill and eat. They hunt everything that moves."

"But how do humans overcome tik-worms?" I ask her.

"Other animals are never able to fight back," says Miki. "But humans are special. The tik-worms can kill the body, can kill the brain, but they cannot kill the human spirit. And in some, the spirit is strong enough to reclaim the body from the worms. Unfortunately, there has yet to be a case where the spirit has fully reclaimed its brain from the worms."

"And the worms keep their flesh alive, even though they don't have control of the body?" I ask.

"The worms stay within their bodies, attempting to reclaim control," says Miki. "They nourish the flesh, keeping the half-dead humans alive, but rarely get the body back."

"In either case," the doctor says, "the tik-worms and the living dead must be destroyed. It makes little difference why or how."

"We need to be quiet," the aquarium/man tells us from the back, dragging Ronald who is coughing through his gag. "The walls are beginning to echo your voices."

Cyn wraps her body around me and licks my wounds.

NUMBER FOURTEEN

"Waspy pork smells, as the hallway goes from shades of blue to deep green . . ."

Echoes up ahead —-> rumbling sounds like screams mixed with hard rain.

"What is it?" Cyn whispers in my ear.

The sound gets louder.

"Something is up there," Miki says.

The aquarium/man barges forward. "No, behind us. They are coming from behind."

We turn. I notice there is another sound coming from far behind us. But not rain-screams. The sound is like stomping footsteps and gargling moans.

"Run," Miki says.

We are unsure which way to run.

"Go, go!" Miki screams, pushing us forward. "They are right behind us!"

Tsuko leads, running with his axe-boomerang behind his shoulder, a sword opening up from his arm like a switchblade. His penis-arm swinging its razor sword in circles.

When we get to the screaming noises, I realize where they are coming from: the walls.

The mouths of the people on the walls are screaming. Human mouths being controlled by the tik-worms. The parasites are shrieking at us, angry with us.

And up ahead, I see we are headed right into a group of shrieking knotty-fleshed undead.

NUMBER FIFTEEN

"Zombie Fight #1 . . ."

There are things I see and don't see. The walls are made of meat and meat juices are dripping on my head and chest. Sweat or blood or something else . . .

There is Tsuko —-> in swirls of movement, cutting down the rotten attackers, several per swing. His limbs are quadruple-jointed and they can bend in every direction without difficulty. He can spin like a windmill and open up heads and torsos, sever arms and legs.

The doctor, Ran, is shooting spiked balls at the zombies behind us, killing the ones in front to slow their path.

Tsuko fights best alone. He is far ahead of us now. He has no trouble destroying zombies on all sides of him at once. Occasionally, he will come back to us and open Miki up from the back and pull out metallic internal organs. Then he'll run back to the zombies to fight them with her guts.

Cyn watches the flashes of movement, hugs/kisses me. She smiles when Tsuko unfolds Miki's internal organs into razor-weapons: her lungs become a battle axe, her spine a spear, her large intestine a razor-wire whip.

Miki is starting to look like an empty paper-mâché doll.

Cyn opens her mouth and catches blood drops on her tongue. "It's fun," she says.

We are totally unaffected by the zombie fight. We are watching a performance of a battle, not at all a part of it. There is nothing to make us feel threatened anymore. We are walking casually through the cold dead bodies, more concerned with slipping on their spilt guts than getting eaten by the dead.

Ronald is even more casual than we are, more calm than he was before the zombies attacked. He is at home with them. His steps just behind ours, hands in his pockets, mind on something more important . . .

NUMBER SIXTEEN

"Dialogue from Zombie Fight #1 . . ."

Do zombies make love?

I'm not sure if their parts work. I think a dead penis won't get hard.

They can use a strap-on dildo.

I don't think they have dildos.

They can use anything long and hard.

Maybe they don't have a sex drive. I don't ever see them having sex.

Look at that one! It has an erection!

Maybe seeing food, our flesh, is sexually exciting to it.

Let's have sex with it.

No, it will eat us.

You're so prejudice. You don't like black hoods, you don't like zombies . . .

They want to eat us!

I want them to eat us. I want them to fuck us and eat us. I want to eat them as they fuck us.

They don't want to fuck. They want to kill.

I want to strap one down and molest it.

I'm disturbed now.

We can fuck right now. On top of all these corpses, on all this juicy meat.

That's not normal. And we are in too much danger for that.

I want a threesome with a zombie.

No.

Threesome!

How about a threesome with the mechanical woman?

We can't.

Why not?

She has a Cunt Of Death™.

What is a Cunt Of Death™?

It is half vagina and half deadly weapon.

That doesn't sound erotic . . .

Its cum is acid and its period is fire.

We should not have threesomes.

Perhaps some other time . . .

There are more zombies up ahead.

A lot of zombies.

They are too many to count. An endless crowd of them in front of us and behind us.

Tsuko must be tired.

There are too many dead zombies clogging the hallway. It will be hard for him to maneuver in all those corpses.

I'm getting hungry. When can we eat?

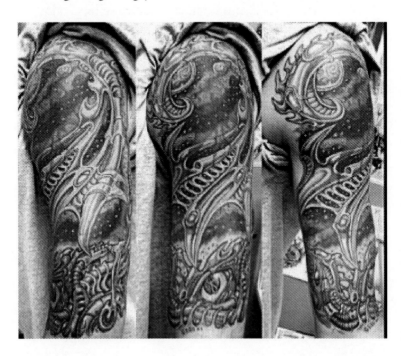

NUMBER SEVENTEEN

"Running through another hallway with the dead surrounding us . . ."

"We are trapped," Miki says.

"No way out," the doctor says.

They are very calm.

I look around. Yes, we are trapped. The walls, floor, ceiling, no passages to escape into.

No, wait.

The ceiling.

Right above me is the little/old girl with half a face crucified to the ceiling. She is coated in nails and still twitching a little.

"This way," I tell the mechanical people.

I lift Cyn on my good shoulder and she unzips the girl from her vagina to her neck, and then climbs in.

One by one, we lift ourselves into the girl's torso, taking the secret passage to my bedroom.

NUMBER EIGHTEEN

"Flickery lights and zombie growls . . ."

We are all just sitting here on my bed, staring at each other. Seven grown people in one bed.

The mechanical people are deep in thought but they don't share their thoughts with me. Ronald sits too close to Cyn, ogling over her with his scabby eyeballs. His face is all wrecked/litter-boxed from the tik-worms. Cyn's patchwork flesh looks natural compared to what the parasites did to him.

"What do we do now?" I ask everyone.

They don't seem to hear my words.

Miki makes clothes for Cyn out of a sheet, but Cyn doesn't like it. She wears only a few strands of the outfit for decoration.

I rub my fingers across her patterned arm and she smiles at me.

"You should rest," the doctor tells me. "This might be the only chance you get."

I nod and Cyn has already cleared a spot in her lap for me to lay my head. She stares at me when I go to sleep. I can feel her licking things while drifting in and out of consciousness.

NUMBER NINETEEN

"Spidery dreams that make my brain rough and sticky inside my skull..."

I awake. My eyes are glued shut. I am covered in a sticky liquid that smells like blood.

but —> ...

Gnarling voices all around me, rumbling the walls, like I am being eaten alive by the living dead.

Prying my eyes open: Cyn...

She is smearing blood on me. Pieces of flesh are in her hands and she rubs them all over her naked body, then on my naked body. Growling with the undead outside of my bedroom.

"What happened?" the mechanical people wake from meditation positions and scream at me. "What has she done?"

Cyn has killed and eaten the other human, Ronald. A crazed killer but still a human being...

"I was sooo hungry," Cyn says, chewing on scrotum skin, bloody bag, a testicle dangling out of the sack.

"Life is precious!" the mechanical people scream. "Life is precious! Life is precious!"

The corpse is in pieces and we are all coated in them.

Miki picks up Ronald's severed head, half its face has been removed, blood dribbles out of the neck...

"Can he be fixed?" Miki asks the doctor.

"She has digested too much," the doctor replies.

"This is murder," Miki says. "She does what the zombies do."

"Yet you don't stop her from eating?" I say.

"She should eat quickly," they tell me. "Every drop of blood should be gone or the dead will smell us."

"Eat, eat," Cyn says to me, putting flesh pieces into my face until I shove them away.

"We all must help," says the mechanical people. "She is almos full."

They cut the corpse into chunks and shovel his meat into the doctor's thigh cabinets. They put some of his meat down my throat. try not to taste it or throw up. Cyn licks the blood off of everyone unti we are safe . . .

NUMBER TWENTY

"Halfway between dreams and a conversation . . ."

"We might have to put her to sleep."
    "Yes, she killed a perfectly functional man."
    "Mostly functional . . ."
    "She should be destroyed."
    "But life is precious . . ."
    "But she does not treat life preciously."
    "She should be dealt with."
    "She should be preserved."
    "Maybe we could punish her."
    "She should be killed once we get back to the ship."
    "Or perhaps before then."
    "It is settled, we will kill her."
    "But not yet."
    "Soon, not now."
    "What about killing her now?"
    "No, later."
    "Later is better than now."
    "Well, sometimes now is better than later . . ."
    "Yes, there are times when waiting is a bad thing."
    "We should kill her now."
    "She might kill the other man."
    "The other man's death would be a tragedy."
    "All death is a tragedy . . ."
    "Life is precious."
    "Yes."
    "Death to those who don't believe life is precious."
    "We better not kill her now."

"What if we kill her now?"
"The man might become angry."
"And not come with us."
"Not so loud, he might be awake."
"No, he looks asleep."
"He has to go with us. There is no other way."
"We will have to be very careful about killing her."
"He should think it was by mistake."
"Yes, once we get to the ship we will find a way."
"Are you sure he is asleep?"
"He looks asleep."
"The woman is definitely asleep."
"She is asleep."
"But the man?"
"He does not respond to our conversation."
"He is awake!"
"He moved!"
"No, that was his eye twitching."
"He is asleep."
"We should not disturb him."
"Are you sure he is not awake?"
"Don't touch him."
"Leave them alone."

PART THREE
Pretty Deaths

NUMBER ONE

"Blood-soaked sticky puke bed . . ."

Waking to silent serious-faces:
"What is wrong?" I ask the mechanical people.
"We think the zombies might be gone," Miki says.
Cyn rubs her hands between my arms and chest.
"Go see," Miki tells the scout, Akira.
The aquarium/man nods his tangled face and stands from the bed. He opens a small plug on his belly and the water flushes out of him onto the floor. His skin is hollowing.
Halfway down, Miki plugs his belly button to stop the water. Splashing in his chest ——> the fish inside him are crowded in the shallow water, squirming in his crotch and thighs.
There is now a puddle on the floor. It moves across the ground like it has a mind of its own.
His face has an empty look. There is more character in the water puddle, as it drains through the cracks under the door.

Miki removes Akira's head and slips out an extendable fish net from his throat.
"Are you hungry?" she asks me, probing the aquarium/torso with the fish net. Akira's lifeless head dangles over his back.
I don't nod, but she jerks out a blood-red fish for me and snaps it dead against her steel belly. She offers it to me and I guess I have to accept, slippery in my palm, not sure what to do with it.
"You eat it," she tells me.
"I've never eaten a fish before," I reply.
"It will help your strength. Eat it."
I examine it carefully.

Cyn takes it from me.

"That is not for you," Miki yells at Cyn.

Cyn uses the bird skull knife to cut the fish into pieces for me. She sits on my lap and feeds me the tiny pieces, licking her fingers and my lips after every bite.

And she steals pieces for herself when Miki's back is turned.

NUMBER TWO

"Water is leaking under the door and into the room . . ."

It puddles into a circle around Akira's feet.

Miki unplugs the belly button of the half-empty aquarium anc the water swims up the torso inside, refilling the glass body. Once the aquarium/body is full, Akira comes back to life. He re-plugs himsel and I feel guilty about the fish carcass in my hands.

Akira glares at me with evil machine eyes. I can't bring mysel to even apologize, looking away from him to Cyn —->

Cyn smiles fishy-breathed at me.

"The dead are gone," Akira says.

"Completely?" Miki asks.

"The entire floor was empty."

"They must be going after the commander," Ran says.

Miki raises her eyebrows at the doctor. "You and Tsuko shoulc take the humans to the ship now. Akira and I will go after Ryo."

"We shouldn't split up," Ran says.

"The commander will die if we wait until later."

"Then we should leave immediately."

And the mechanical people look at me, expecting some sort o response.

I just divert my eyes.

Cyn pinches her nipple in my direction . . .

NUMBER THREE

"Silence and ugly . . ."

We are in a hallway.

Green eyeballs form in the flesh walls. They make Cyn squeeze her fists and bite into my neck.

The mechanical people jump at her, but I wave them back.

"She's only scared," I tell them.

"The left passage is secure," Akira says to Ran. "Go that way to the roof. The roof is safe from the dead. Go there."

Miki is already charging the other direction.

"Hurry, hurry, hurry," she says to Akira.

Akira rubs the doctor's wooden shoulder. "Go save them. We will meet up there later."

And then Akira's glass chest explodes, dumping his aquarium insides all over the floor.

NUMBER FOUR

"Shards of glass in my sweaty forehead and Cyn digging her nails into my back . . ."

Eruptions from all sides of the hallways, arms breaking through the fleshy walls and thrashing at us.

A zombie is behind Akira, its arm through his torso.

"Hurry, hurry, hurry," Miki screams.

"Go to safety," Akira mumbles to the doctor as his water drains out of him. Fish flopping on the rot-caked ground, wanting to go back in his chest.

The zombie punches the aquarium into tiny shards as smaller zombies chomp their teeth at floppy fish.

And soon the entire hallway has refilled with the living dead.

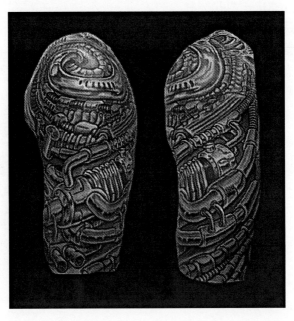

NUMBER FIVE

"Zombie Fight #2 . . ."

"Get them to safety," Miki screams from the other side of the zombie horde.

Tsuko lunges in front of us and pushes me back. His blades dicing the meat from the dead, using his arms like a blender and shredding zombies into smelly bits.

Miki screams out. Her words are not clear under the zombie moaning.

"She's trapped!" Cyn cries.

Miki is backed against a wall, zombies crowding against her, not enough space for her to attack.

"Don't worry!" the doctor yells, pulling on Cyn and pushing me forward. "Forget about her."

Cyn resists him, her patchwork flesh stretching in his grasp.

"Miki," she screams, "use your Cunt Of Death™!"

The doctor pulls Cyn away, giving us distance from the zombie fight.

We hear an explosion.

The zombies are on fire. Miki is shooting flames from her Cunt Of Death™ at them, mad-screaming at their burning meat.

Cyn cheers for Miki, clapping, applauding. The doctor needs to pick her off the ground to get her to move.

Just before she goes out of sight, I see Miki naked from her waste down. Masturbating violently at the zombies. Rubbing her Cunt Of Death™ on them and melting their faces with her acid cum.

NUMBER SIX

"Dialogue from Zombie Fight #2 . . ."

I had a dream last night that you got in a fight with Miki's cunt.
    A what?
    It was an odd dream. Miki challenged you to a duel and it was your idea to fight with your cunts.
    But Miki has a Cunt Of Death™? I wouldn't stand a chance.
    She didn't shoot fire or acid or anything.
    Did I think it was sexual?
    You got into it but Miki was trying to hurt you. She slammed her metal vagina into you until you exploded with blood.
    Did I have an orgasm?
    I think so. It was a bloody orgasm.
    Why did Miki want to fight me?
    Miki wants to kill you for eating Ronald.
    But Ronald was excited for me to eat him.
    All the mechanical people are angry. They want to kill you.
    They won't kill me. They are protecting me. See. Look, they want me to live.
    They say they will eventually kill you but I won't let them.
    Well, if they kill me you can just make me again. You can rebuild me like you did before.
    How do you know so much about everything? How do you know I made you? I never said I did. You know many things I did not tell you.
    I was alive before you made me.
    Alive?
    I was a shadow child.
    ?

Shadow children are similar to what you people call *ghosts*.

So you were once a human like me?

No. Shadow children are the descendants of ghosts.

?

Some humans become ghosts after they die. And ghosts sometimes fall in love and get married. And they can have children together, shadow children. Like me. And shadow children can marry other shadow children and make more shadow children. In fact, I've never even met a ghost that was once a human before. My parents and grandparents were all born in the ghost world.

How did you become alive? Why did you become the wife I created?

I don't know. I was riding a daddy long legs spider in a shadowy corner and the next thing I know I am inside a bucket of meat. And slowly, you turned me into your woman wife. It was very sweet of you.

I've never heard of shadow children.

Humans see very little of the ghost world, which is sad because it is a beautiful place. Much more beautiful than this world.

So does this mean even if we die we can stay together as ghosts?

No, that would be impossible.

Why?

You wouldn't understand the ghost world. Things are complicated.

But why can't we be together? You said people fall in love there.

But new ghosts do not have sex with older ghosts. It is against the rules.

There are rules?

New ghosts are gross. And their minds and sex organs aren't developed yet. You will be like a baby to me.

But don't you love me?

I love you now. I Love being alive with you. But I won't love you anymore if you die.

How can you just stop loving me?

When we are dead I will pretend I don't even know you.

All I wanted was to die with someone I loved. But now you are saying I will be a ghost and you can't love me as a ghost?

Well, you might not even become a ghost. It is very rare for a human to become a ghost after death, in fact.

What will humans become if they don't become ghosts?

I don't know. Nobody knows. Maybe they go to Heaven. It is a philosophical thing and we always hate talking about philosophical things.

What do you mean by *we*? All the ghost people?

No. Me and Rassolf.

Who is Rassolf?

He is my husband.

Your husband?

We were riding on top of a cute daddy long legs spider at the time and both ended up as your wife.

There are two shadow children in you?

Actually, we are one now. Somehow you mixed our souls together into one. We are also combined with the artificial soul that you made for your wife.

Why didn't you tell me this before?

I can't believe I'm telling you this now. I planned on keeping it a secret until after we died.

When you die will your souls become separated again?

I don't know. Maybe we are stuck this way forever.

So what does the ghost world look like?

Like a bird's nest and blue water, but everywhere.

What do you mean?

I've tickled your feet once before.

What?

When I was a ghost. I was in your bedroom and tickled your feet while you were sleeping. And I crawled up and down your leg until you blushed.

Who did this? You or your husband? Or the daddy long legs spider?

Actually, I don't remember . . .

NUMBER SEVEN

"Bloody nose and Cyn with sweat that smells different on each variety of her skin collection . . ."

We stop running once the moans behind us subside, far enough away from the undead to rest.

It is just Cyn, the doctor, and myself now.

A puddle of water is flowing towards us, but the doctor won't admit that it is Akira. "He is lost to us," Ran says. "Keep going."

He leads us to a quiet room at the end of the hallway and breaks the lock off of a door.

"What are you doing?" I ask him. "We're supposed to go to the roof."

"We have to wait for Tsuko," he tells me, opening the door to lean his wooden chest on its splintery parts.

"Why did we leave Tsuko anyway?"

"He fights better alone. For now, we must keep—"

We see something in Ran's eyes as he looks into the room. Something that paralyzes him.

"What is it?" Cyn asks.

He just shakes his head. Can't speak.

I peek over his shoulder. The room is bright and alive. Alien. I can't get a good look around Ran's bushy-crazed hair. But it must be something grotesque.

Behind us: a screech of the walking dead.

And the doctor breaks his trance.

Zombies are all around us.

"We have to go inside," he tells us, cracky voice. "We have no choice."

He pushes Cyn and I into the room first. As if he feels safer with the living dead.

Inside ——-> a tik-worm city. An intricate work of architecture made from metal and human flesh.

And there's people here.

No. Parts of people . . .

There are body parts walking on their own. A leg with a head on top of it hopping across the room. A torso with dozens of fingers attached, like a fat centipede crawling up the flesh wall.

A lively city of squishy creations. My eyes go dizzy from all the activity, all the fat-bubbling sounds.

"Move slowly," Ran says as he leads us through.

I try not to look at the gyrating mutations. I turn to Cyn for maybe a smile or hand-squeeze but she is ripping a chunk of flesh from the floor and bringing it to her mouth.

"Don't!" I scream at her, jerking the meat from her hand. "It's infested with diseases and tik-worms."

Cyn with angry lips. She takes a bite of the meat and throws it at my face, stuns me. And she lifts her hand, about to smack me in the face.

But zombies burst into the room, breaking her concentration.

"Quickly," Ran yells.

We fumble through the slippery meat castles to him on the far side of the room, avoiding twisty flesh-creatures.

"There!" Ran points to a door at the far end of the room.

I lunge forward, grabbing Cyn's wrist tight and pulling her over the meat cities to Ran.

The door opens up to a staircase and we climb.

Just before closing the door, Ran is again paralyzed with amazement, or is it fear? This time, on the staircase, I can see over him. I can see all the squishy creatures attacking the zombies. Grabbing them. Biting them. Tearing them down.

"Miki was right," the doctor tells us. "The zombies were not created by the parasites."

His mechanical eyes click-click-click as the closing door squeezes us into darkness.

NUMBER EIGHT

"Hiding in a musty storage loft that hasn't been used in a hundred years . . ."

"Ryo, Ryo," the doctor resonates into his communication device. There isn't a response.

He rubs red sweat out of his scraggled hair.

Again into his device, "Miki, Miki."

No response.

A puddle of water creeps up the stairs to us. Cyn smiles and pinches my back skin.

"Miki, Miki," Ran screams into his device. "Miki, Miki!"

Cyn presses her face against the warm liquid swirling at our feet. She mmmmmms bubbles in the water and licks her lips.

"Pilot Yuta, Pilot Yuta," Ran paces in the background. "Yuta, Yuta, where are you?"

"Akira's here," Cyn tells the doctor. And then she puts her face back into the puddle and slurps the fluid.

"Tsuko, Tsuko, Tsuko!" Ran closes his eyes tight and tosses the communicator away. Plops down hard, vibrating the loft.

"None of them are responding," the doctor tells me.

"Are they dead?" I ask.

"They are not responding," he says.

Cyn is sprawled across the floor, licking the dusty liquid, rubbing against the wet.

The liquid tries to swim away from her, but she is too quick. It tries climbing up her throat, but she can swallow hard and hold the water down until it is absorbed into her.

And Cyn licks her patchwork lips.

"What do we do now?" I ask the doctor.

He is sitting there. Awkward-slouching, staring at the ground.

Then wheels extend out of Ran's thighs.

"Stay . . . stay . . . stay . . ." he says, as he rolls back slowly into the shadows.

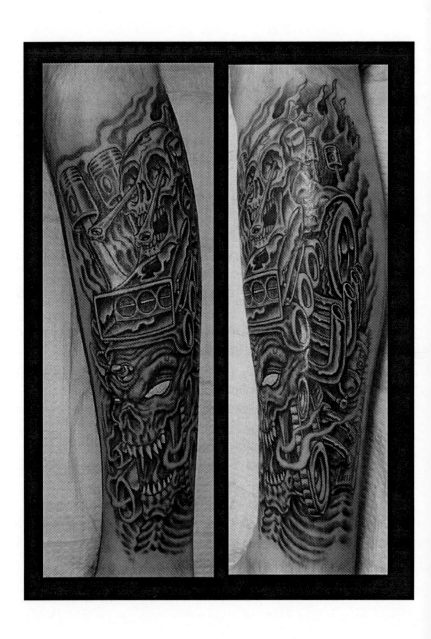

NUMBER NINE

"The door bursts open . . ."

A bloody mangled mass struggles up the steps and leaps near my feet, collapsing me to the ground. I kick it with the heels of my feet but they just clay-squish into the intruder, forming around its gnarled parts.

Cyn pulls me back and I scurry-stand before it gets the chance to grab me.

"Tsuko!" Ran howls from the shadows, rolling out to help the pile of bloody mess.

I rub my eyes until I can see clearly.

"I figured you were lost to us," Ran tells Tsuko and Cyn sits next to him stroking glassy features.

The doctor goes right to work on Tsuko, screwing limbs back together and adding supports to his joints.

"Can you put him back together?" I ask. "Like you did before."

"It is more serious this time," the doctor says. "Many vital parts have been eaten off of him.

The doctor's face freezes. Then sinks.

"What?" I ask, jabbing him on his wooden shoulder until I get a splinter.

"He leaks mind fluid," the doctor cries.

"What's that mean?"

"It means he will die. There is no way to save him."

"How long does he have?"

"Twenty minutes. Maybe."

I look to Cyn and squeeze her ankle. She is chewing a wound on her thigh.

"We have to go," Ran says. "Right now."

"Now?" Cyn says. "You said we could rest."

"Tsuko has very little time left. We need him to get to the roof. He will be useless to us if we wait any longer."

I look at the fighter on the ground. He is curled up and coughing up greasy blood.

"He doesn't look like he'll be any help at all," I say. "We should let him die in peace."

"No," says the doctor. "He wants to die with honor. He will use the last of his life to save others."

"You decide for him?"

"I decide nothing. It is the way of our people."

"Who are you people anyway?"

"We are the saviors of Earth."

"Saviors? Says who?"

"It is our destiny to return peace to the world. Even if it means our death."

"He should be able to choose."

"He doesn't have a choice."

Tsuko staggers to his feet and swings blades out of his arms as a salute to the doctor. His cock-hand also draws a razor axe and salutes.

"Ready?" Ran asks the fighter.

Tsuko is swaying, a stream of orange fluid drips down his neck and chest.

"We go now," the doctor tells me, pulling claw weapons out of his chest drawer and attaching them to his hands. The claws are long, thin razors, shiny, almost glowing in the shadows of the loft.

NUMBER TEN

"We charge through the room of fleshies, slippery and avoiding contact with tik-worms . . ."

Tsuko moves drunkenly, slicing up meaty creatures that get in his way. He is not as precise and catlike anymore. But his attacks are still explosive and scatter flesh around like rose petals.

Out into the hallway, the zombies are already gathered to greet us.

"Almost there," the doctor says to me.

I grab the doctor by the shoulder.

"You're not going to do anything to Cyn when we get to the roof, are you?"

"What do you mean?" he asks.

Tsuko is already charging sloppily into combat with the undead.

"I heard you all talking about killing her after you got me to the ship."

"Oh, yes." He smiles at me. "Yes, yes." And he turns back to the dead.

"No!" I tell him, jerking him back to me.

"Must be done," he says, breaking my hold and charging into the horde with claw-blades stretching the width of the hallway.

NUMBER ELEVEN

"ZOMBIE FIGHT #3 . . ."

The doctor and Tsuko dancing . . .

A squishy attack dance.

Cyn and I take no part in it. We are naked together, kissing sometimes, no music to dance to. The dead wish the mechanical people had more meat in them. Less metal . . . A corpse bites into Tsuko's metal wrist and the teeth begin to chip apart.

"We'll never get to the roof," I tell the Cyn-licks on my chest. "There's too many dead people and Tsuko is weak. The doctor is even weaker."

We follow the mechanical soldiers through the zombies, stepping over the pieces of undead as we go.

Tsuko is sloppy. His blades are aiming for zombie torsos and not the heads. The zombies keep getting mangled into bloody strings before Tsuko gets around to killing their brains.

The doctor seems to be more concentrated on dodging Tsuko's blades than killing zombies. He is very anal with his steps.

But we are still moving forward.

We are still breaking through.

And the corpse pieces are piling up. The farther we move, the higher the flesh pile builds up. We are moving at a slant now, hiking up a hill. Dead rotten body parts under my feet.

NUMBER TWELVE

"Dialogue from Zombie Fight #3 . . ."

It's my birthday today.

Happy birthday!

It's not really my birthday today . . .

Oh . . .

When I was a kid I decided to make everyday my birthday.

Every single day?

I always feel sad when it's not my birthday so I wanted it to always be my birthday.

I didn't get you a present.

That's okay. I've never gotten a present before.

I don't know when my birthday is. Shadow children don't follow any calender.

That's a shame. Birthdays are great. People treat you nice.

I've gotten presents before. One time Rassolf gave me a snail ring.

Did it make you happy?

Oh, yes.

Why snail?

Snails make the best dreams.

?

In the shadows, we are able to watch the dreams of others through their skin. Thoughts and dreams are projected out of every pore in the body. Our culture revolves around watching others' dreams, whether they be humans or ghosts or animals or plants. Everything can dream. But snails dream the best.

I wish I could see the ghost world.

Maybe you will someday.

I don't want to die anymore.

I want to be eaten alive by zombies while you fuck me.

No, I want to die peacefully in your arms, not painfully and violently.

You will most likely die violently and painfully. Wouldn't you rather be having sex when you die? Violence and pain makes sex more intense.

I don't think I'd be able to have an orgasm.

I'm having an orgasm just thinking about it . . .

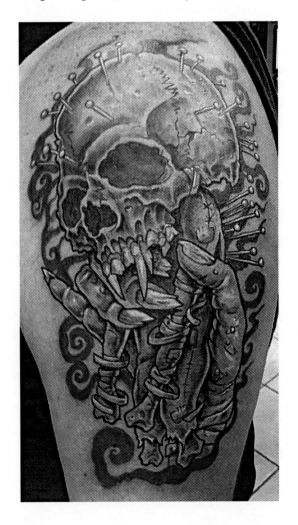

NUMBER THIRTEEN

"Piled up dead zombies all the way to the ceiling . . ."

So we have to crawl between ceiling and corpse parts. Tsuko up ahead killing more zombies, his limbs folded inwards, a mechanical spider. And all the zombies behind us lack the ability to climb.

By the time we reach the hatch to the roof, we no longer need to climb a ladder to get through it. Though the mechanical people do have to pull us through the tight spaces, our flesh saturated in zombie juice. Cyn becomes aroused by the dead-meat smell.

Outside --->
The sky is a swirl of colors. Purple, orange, red, green. Mostly dark purple and orange. Twilight. The blobby sun already over the horizon.

A green-ice wind freezes my sweat.

I am busy pushing Cyn away from the rot-fluids on me when the doctor opens a drawer on his chest and hands me an axe.

Not just any axe, but my exquisite antique axe.

"Why?" I ask him, but the answer to that question is right in front of us.

The roof is occupied by an army of dead ones. With insecty eyes on me, only me.

"We've got a long way to the ship," the doctor says, pointing to a metal object in the distance. "You might need to defend yourself. Don't use it unless absolutely necessary."

And he gives Cyn my bird skull knife.

I imagined the axe in my hand would give me a sense of security. But it did quite the opposite. The weapon in my hand is causing panic. I am not the mechanical people's safe little treasure anymore. I am on my own. Left to defend myself from hordes of zombies.

Cyn bites her knife in excitement. She is steaming hot, licking motley lips at me.

"Tsuko is going to cut a path to the ship," Ran says. "Once is is open, I will lead you through. Keep going until you reach the ship. If we separate do not stop."

"Sexy," Cyn tells me.

She doesn't explain what is sexy.

Tsuko is off, throwing boomerang/blade weapons that fly from his fists, kill some zombies, and return to him as fast as wind. Several of the dead have fallen before he even reaches the army. His cock's axe thrashing through the lifeless attackers cutting them open while his upper arms swing warhammers and catch/throw boomerang blades at the dead.

He is utterly out of control.

He seems to be several machines at once, a walking meat grinder mixed with a wood chipper.

"Go, go," the doctor says, catching me off guard.

Tsuko has already made a path for us. We are running. Cyn gropes against my back and licks/bites my neck. She wants to be eaten alive. She doesn't want escape. Just wants to fuck me dead.

The path has gotten pretty small once we reach it. I hold my axe at the zombies I pass. I should swing, but I don't want to dull the blade. It is freshly sharpened.

Tsuko is staggering. His brain fluid must be almost out. He stops defending himself from the dead. Just standing. Trying to hold himself from falling down.

"No, Tsuko, not yet," the doctor screams, far ahead of Cyn and I. "We're not there yet!"

And Tsuko brings himself back together, swinging his sword blindly.

While we pass him, I feel safety. The eye of a tornado. But it only lasts a moment before heading back into the storm of rotten attackers.

Cyn has stopped groping me.

She is running by my side, licking me only slightly when I bump into her.

We are just about clear of the zombie ocean. Only a few more feet . . .

Tsuko's blade cuts open my back.

"Tsuko!" Ran screams as all of my muscles seize up and I crumple to the blooded concrete.

Staring up at the purple-orange sky. It begins to rain. For a moment, I feel the rain is several varieties of house paint. And the colors from the sky are leaking onto us. Making me orange, purple, red, and green speckled. A living human-shaped Jackson Pollack painting. My hair is glued to my neck. My thoughts are draining out of the chasm in my back . . .

Cyn drops on top of me and drinks from my wound. I can feel very little of her tongue.

The doctor runs at me in slow motion.

I turn to Tsuko. His cock-arm has been ripped out of him and he has dropped all weapons. By the time Ran gets to him he is on the ground. All the life drained out pooling on the concrete.

I can only hear my own breath now. And the vibrating rain against my spine. Cyn's arms wrapped around me only hurts a few parts of my skin.

She is covered in blood.

"Let's fuck," Cyn says. "Now's our chance."

I think I groan at her.

"Go," Ran screams at Cyn. "Get him to the ship!"

Cyn actually listens. Helps me up and drags me through the corpses. Maybe she knows I am unable to have sex. I can't feel anything in my penis.

The doctor shoots spiked steel balls into the zombies near us but we are mostly free of the zombies and stumbling towards the silver airship —> a turtle-shaped vehicle with wings, covered in razor spikes.

We are here, finally safe, collapsing against the door of the ship.

"How do we get it open?" Cyn asks, sagging me to the ground.

I just lie here, watching the rickety corpses against the swirl-colored twilight.

I see the doctor cutting Tsuko's torso with his claw blades, splitting it open.

The corpses are all over him, lunging over his back at him as he pulls out pieces of Tsuko's meat.

There is something inside of Tsuko that the doctor wants . . .

He pulls on it, but the zombies have him at the joints and they are digging into Tsuko to get to his very few meat parts.

The doctor pulls, cutting at the zombies. And the object gives, slides out of Tsuko's torso.

Ran holds it over his head:
A chainsaw made of glass.

The doctor pulls a chord and the glass chainsaw's blades begin to whir. It makes a high-pitched sound, a crystal humming noise that overwhelms me.

It blocks out the sound of the zombie growls anymore.

Then the doctor lowers the glass chainsaw into a zombie in front of him. And with very little strength, the zombie is split in half. Smooth. Like cutting cheese.

And the doctor gives them a mad grin. His hair is wild with dried blood.

He is able to cut down all of the dead coming at him, slicing off heads, cutting them through the middle, or sometimes he halves them vertically.

"We can't get in," Cyn cries to him.

The doctor acknowledges and comes charges over her, spin-opening dead ones along the way.

He arrives out of breath, his wooden torso chipped and splintered. One drawer is missing completely.

After tapping some buttons on one of the ship's spikes, a door swings open to glowy lights and beep-sounds.

He helps me up with his coarse shoulder and gets me into the ship, laying me onto a metal-mash floor.

Outside, he faces Cyn with a cold glare.

"Not you," he says.

And he swings at Cyn's legs with the glass chainsaw.

It cuts through her thighs, severing them clean. And she hits the concrete ass-first. Her legs still standing in front of her, bleeding.

She doesn't scream.

Maybe I can't hear her cries over my own screaming.

And the doctor just smiles at me as the ship door closes between us, separating me from them.

Me from my love.

NUMBER FOURTEEN

"Somebody hates me today. Is it God? I guess it might as well be God..."

I'm bleeding all over the place and can hardly move.

I hear Cyn screaming outside. Imagining her legs still standing by themselves next to her.

The room I'm in, the room in the ship, is cluttered with chirpy lights and orange shadows. I crawl on the floor for a while. Then I stop. I don't know where I'm going. What do I do now?

Looking for a way to open the door to bring legless Cyn inside. But I do not see any doorknobs. I hit a panel of lights that might be buttons. The door doesn't open. I try some lever-things, try talking into an intercom-type box, even try opening and closing my eyes really fast. The door won't budge.

Cyn cries some more.

I cry for Cyn.

We are both going to bleed to death and we don't even have each other to die with. I'd rather be ripped apart by zombies like she wanted. We would have gone out with an explosion of sex and death.

Now, even if I get outside to her we are too mutilated to perform sex properly.

I need to get her inside.

NUMBER FIFTEEN

"Struggling to open the door and bleeding and crying sometimes . . ."

Cyn's screams have faded already, but I am still trying. She might still have a little life left. Just enough to die with.

Ticky-crab noises behind me.

But I don't want to look. Turning my neck will destroy my back. Make my body spasm and hurt.

More tick-tick-tick noises. Scrambling ticks.

All around me.

Zombies? Trying to get in?

And then a giant bug lands in my lap.

My nerves explode in my skin and for a moment I forget my back is wide open and leap across the metal floor.

A dozen of them.

No. More. Much more . . .

Mechanical bugs bigger than dolls.

They scurry at me with tick-tick-ticking noises. Like little wind-up toys.

I try to get away from them but I can't feel parts of my body anymore. I am dizzy. The insects are creeping through pools of my blood.

The room is starting to look fluffy to me. Almost liquid.

And the floor is coming at me really *really* fast.

NUMBER SIXTEEN

"Waking . . ."

Cyn leaning over me, so close I can see nothing but her skin-collage face. Her lips big and detailed and quivering at me.

"Are we dead?" I ask.

"No," she whispers. "I can't see your dreams."

She steps back and I see a body on her that is not hers.

"What happened?"

She rubs her new mechanical legs, black and shiny. Many levers and gadgets entwined within. "We are like the others now."

Mechanical.

I examine Cyn more closely:

Metal weapons have been woven into her flesh. Hook-like fins go up her arms and legs. Her head is growing machinery for hair. Fingernails now crude knives. And I think she even has vampire teeth.

"What did they do to you? They made you a machine."

"You should see yourself." She smiles and licks her lips with a long razor tongue.

I sit up.

I am on an operating table. In a small room with three other tables and a lot of blank space. A bookcase crowded with more mechanical bugs, smiling at us, waiting for something else to do.

"Look." Cyn points her mirror-plated ass at me.

I see my reflection. I don't recognize myself.

I look almost like Akira, like an aquarium/man. But not an aquarium. My skin is painted with a happy blue sky. But the painting moves.

They turned my body into a television screen. A beautiful land scape with clouds moving and wind rustling yellow-green trees. A few birds are flying around in the distance.

"What am I?" I ask Cyn's ass-mirror.

"I don't know." She sits next to me. "But you are beautiful."

She rubs my movie skin and licks the grass.

I watch her watching me.

There is a small door on the side of her head.

"Where does that lead to?" I ask.

Cyn slaps her head-door. "Oh, look!"

She opens up her skull to show me a small version of herself inside. It is exactly like the pre-mechanical Cyn, but with wings. Like a fairy.

The two Cyns smile at each other and lick each other's patch-work lips.

Then the mini-Cyn's wings flutter like a hummingbird and she takes off. Exploring the small room in jerky dart-like flights.

NUMBER SEVENTEEN

"I can feel the landscape inside of my torso. Feel the wind blowing, trees rustling, the warmth of the sun, like the insides of my body have really become a miniature landscape . . ."

We wait for someone to come get us. Nobody comes. I wonder if Ran died out there. I wonder if Miki ever made it to her commander. If everyone is dead . . .

There is no one else here in the ship. Just us, alone. So we leave. We wander the ship.

It is much larger than it appeared outside. Doors take us hours to figure out. Every knob turns differently. It holds up our exploration and makes Cyn stamp her metal feet.

But the rooms we go through are worth the wait. They are not all blank/empty. Most are colorful and overwhelming. We find a room with a bright yellow tree that coos glowing bubbles at us. There is a room with jelly-flavored furniture. A room that makes you feel under-water with skull-shaped fish. Another containing a playground full of slugs and an apple tree.

It takes us an entire day to get to the bridge.

"We need food," Cyn says.

"I'm not hungry at all," I tell her.

"Neither am I. But I need to eat anyway."

NUMBER EIGHTEEN

"On the bridge, a pilot's corpse . . ."

He looks like a porcupine of machine and flesh. His fists holding a knife inside of his guts and innards are in a pile on the floor.

"We are trapped here," I say, scratching a tree on my chest. The tree's bark is making me itchy.

We can see outside of the ship. The landscape is dim and slime-foggy. There aren't any signs of zombies or tik-worm flesh creatures. Just a cold dead world.

"If only we knew how to fly this thing . . ." I look at Cyn and smile but she is busy glaring at the pilot's guts. The fairy version of herself sitting on her shoulder.

"Where is there to go?" Cyn puts her miniature self back into her head.

"We wouldn't need a place. We'd just go."

We hear banging outside of the ship. It started as background noise and I didn't notice it. Now it is louder.

"We could find adventure out there."

Hundreds of fists hammering against the hull.

"We could find paradise. A place of peace and happiness."

Twisting moan-sounds. Angry growls.

"We could find more people. Maybe a society that still exists."

Claws on metal sounds . . .

"We could go to the sky. Fly above the clouds. Make love in the stars. Maybe even circle the Earth. See if we can find out if Heaven is really out there . . ."

We smile at each other.
Then stare at the controls of the ship and pretend we know how to use them.

THE END

ABOUT THE AUTHOR

Carlton Mellick III decided to become an author at the early age of 10, just after giving up his previous life-long dream of becoming grand master of 'Moon Patrol' for the Atari 2600. He writes 3-4 novel-like things a year, including RAZOR WIRE PUBIC HAIR, SATAN BURGER, TEETH AND TONGUE LANDSCAPE, and the upcoming PUNK LAND. His shorter works have appeared in over 80 publications including RAN-DOM ACTS OF WEIRDNESS, STRANGEWOOD TALES, and most recently THE YEAR'S BEST FAN-TASY AND HORROR 16. He currently resides in Portland, OR, where he makes a homemade pizza known as 'The Glogulator.,' a concotion that contains but is not limited to bratwurst, sauerkraut, pineapple, and habanero peppers.

Visit him online at: www.AVANTPUNK.com

ABOUT THE COVER/TATTOO ARTIST

Pooch has been a tattoo artist since 1994, and has been drawing since he was a child. The discovery of digital software such as Bryce and photoshop opened him up to new worlds that could be quickly realized in cyberspace at the click of a mouse. Pooch explored this medium for a few years and decided to move on to traditional painting methods. Raised on a diet of Walt Disney World, Ray Harryhausen films, Florida tiki tourist traps and more recently, tattoo imagery, Pooch paints images that seem to exist in a bizarre Afterlife. His art is a visual cocktail mix of Far East mysteries, Western mythology Mexican day of the dead imagery with a shot of tattoo culture, shaken and stirred, and served up in a souvenir tiki skull. Pooch cites diverse influences such as H.R. Giger, Pushead, Robert Williams, Ernst Fuchs, Tim Burton, Juenet and Caro, Todd Schorr, Mark Ryden, Jecek Yerka and Antoni Gaudi. Pooch's paintings have been featured in Tattoo Revue, International Tattoo Art, and Tattoo Savage.

WWW.POOCHISLAND.COM

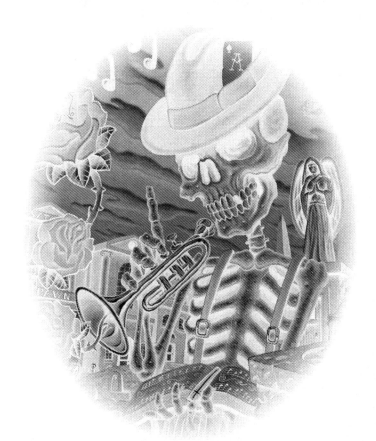

TATTOOS
●
ARTWERKS
BY POOCH

ERASERHEAD PRESS

www.eraserheadpress.com

Eraserhead Press is a collective publishing organization with a mission to create a new genre for "bizarre" literature. A genre that brings together the neo-surrealists, the post-postmodernists, the literary punks, the magical realists, the masters of grotesque fantasy, the bastards of offbeat horror, and all other rebels of the written word. Together, these authors fight to tear down convention, explode from the underground, and create a new era in alternative literature. All the elements that make independent films "cult" films are displayed twice as wildly in this fiction series. Eraserhead Press strives to be your major source for bizarre cult fiction.

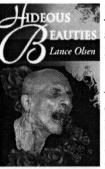

HIDEOUS BEAUTIES

stories by Lance Olsen (images by Andi Olsen)
208 pages / $13.95 / ISBN 0-9729598-0-7

A collection of a dozen outrageous fictions, each based
on a photograph, painting, sketch, collage, or assemblage by an equally outrageous artist (Hans Bellmer,
Ed Kienholz, Joel-Peter Witkin, et alia), that explores
the amphibious edge where language and image splice.

RAZOR WIRE PUBIC HAIR

an illustrated novel by Carlton Mellick III
176 pages / $10.95 / ISBN 0-9729598-1-5

A psycho-sexual fairy tale about a multi-gendered scewing toy
purchased by a razor dominatrix and brought into her night-
marish lifestyle of surreal sex and mutilation.

MY DREAM DATE (RAPE)
WITH KATHY ACKER

stories by Michael Hemmingson
176 pages / $10.95 / ISBN 0-9713572-9-3

Sex, drugs, Raymond Carver's ghost, Barbie dolls loving GI Joe dolls, the pure vaginas of French girls, the
un-pure vagina of Kathy Acker, crack whores, nutty
neighbors, scatological girlfriends, iniquitous fiends,
Jesus freaks, pornographers, pushers, movers, shakers
and winning lottery tickets.

SKIN PRAYER

fragments of abject memory by Doug Rice
232 pages / $14.95 / ISBN 0-9713572-7-7

"A series of mysterious and deeply evocative meditations: erotic,
surreal, tender, grave, and profane."

- Carole Maso

STRANGEWOOD TALES

an anthology edited by Jack Fisher
176 pages / $10.95 / ISBN 0-9713572-0-X

Bizarre horror by Kurt Newton, Jeffrey Thomas, Richard Gavin, Charles Anders, Brady Allen, DF Lewis, Carlton Mellick III, Scott Thomas, GW Thomas, Carol MacAllister, Jeff Vandermeer, Monica J. O'Rourke. Gene Michael Higney, Scott Milder, Andy Miller, Forrest Aguirre, Jack Fisher, Eleanor Terese Lohse, Shane Ryan Staley, and Mark McLaughlin.

SHALL WE GATHER AT THE GARDEN?

a novel full of novels by Kevin L. Donihe
248 pages / $14.95 / ISBN 0-9713572-5-0

Have you ever felt dislocated within the world? Did you ever have "one of those days" when everything unravelling before you seems truly bizarre and you begin to question your own sanity? Meet Mark Anders, the #1 bestselling romance writer in America.

SATAN BURGER

an anti-novel by Carlton Mellick III
236 pages / $14.95 / ISBN 0-9713572-3-4

Six squatter punks get jobs at a fast food chain owned by the devil in an apocalyptic godless world.

"It's odd... very crass... vulgar... funny... and just all around easy and delightful to read." - *Nacho Cheese and Anarchy*

ELECTRIC JESUS CORPSE

an anti-novel in 12 parts by Carlton Mellick III
384 pages / $17.95 / ISBN 0-9713572-8-5

The story of the messiah, Jesus Christ, thrown into a surreal and zombie-plagued version of modern day Earth.

"This is one of the most odd, strange, weird books I have ever read, and enjoyed every minute of it." - *Top Site*

SOME THINGS ARE BETTER LEFT UNPLUGGED

a novel by Vincent Sakowski
156 pages / $9.95 / ISBN 0-9713572-2-6

A postmodern fantasy that satirizes many of our everyday obsessions. "Full of images and situations that stretch the imagination." - *PEEP SHOW*

THE KAFKA EFFEKT

stories by D. Harlan Wilson
216 pages / $13.95 / ISBN 0-9713572-1-8

A manic depressive has a baby's bottom grafted onto his face; a hermaphrodite impregnates itself and gives birth to twins; a gaggle of professors find themselves trapped in a port-a-john and struggle to liberate their minds from the prison of reason—these are just a few of the precarious situations that the characters herein are forced to confront.

SKIMMING THE GUMBO NUCLEAR

a novel by M. F. Korn
292 pages / $16.95 / ISBN 0-9713572-6-9

The colorful denizens of the southern delta nether regions of the state of Louisiana are grappling for their very lives as pollution and nuclear waste transform this sportsman's paradise into a grand epic wasteland of surreal pandemic plague.

ALL THE MUTANT TRASH IN ALL THE GALAXIES

4 novels by M. F. Korn
284 pages / $16.95 / ISBN 0-9729598-4-X

Lovesick stalkers, synthetic whores, abused robots, Lolitas, conmen, robber barons, oilfield and nuclear blue collar white trash, schizophrenic aliens, video oulaws, rednecks, thieves, indentured androids, barflies, pharmaceutical overlords, squatters, smut merchants and good country people all carving out a piece of desperate living for themselves in these 4 novels of anti-genre sci-fi.

STRANGER ON THE LOOSE
Stories by D. Harlan Wilson
228 pages / $13.95 / ISBN 0-9729598-3-1

Bodybuilders sneak into people's homes and strike poses at their leisure. Passive-aggressive glaciers and miniature elephant-humans antagonize the seedy streets of Suburbia. Apes disguised as scientists reincarnate Walt Disney, who discovers that he is a Chinese box full of disguised Walt Disneys... Wilson's imagintion is a rare specimen.

ERASERHEAD DOUBLE #1
244 pages / $14.95 / ISBN 0-9729598-6-6

<u>MY FLING WITH BETTY PAGE</u> *by Michael Hemminsgon*
A private eye living in a self-contained alternate universe is hired to find the rare Betty Page stamp, but stumbles on the truth o reality, and the interdimensional aliens who wish to destroy it

<u>YELLOW #10</u> *by Trevor Dodge*
Yellow #10 is a work of experimental fiction that throws Susan and Sharon, those rascally Baby Boomer twins from Disney' *The Parent Trap* full in the throes of a 1990s-style adolescen identity crisis, where anti-depressants, confessional poetry, cry for-help suicides, and the constipated rhythms of pre-teen se: are set to the sticky-sweet backbeat of pre-millennial pop music

ERASERHEAD DOUBLE #2
208 pages / $13.95 / ISBN 0-9729598-8-2

<u>ANGEL SCENE</u> *by Richard Kadrey*
Enter the world of the angels - biologically-engineered killing machines designed to get sexual pleasure from their murders the life of the angels is one intensely erotic and violent escapad after another.

<u>TEETH & TONGUE LANDSCAPE</u> *by Carlton Mellcik III*
In a world made out of meat, a socially-obsessive monophobi man finds himself to be the last human being on the face of th planet. Desperate for social interaction, he explores the land scape of flesh and blood, teeth and tongue, trying to befrien any strange creature or community that he comes across.

.

i-o

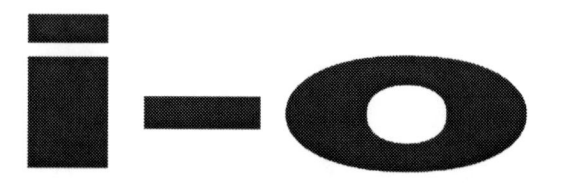

coming soon:

Notes Towards The Design And Production Of The Protohuman

A new short novel from Simon Logan, author of I-O

MY NAME IS DZIGA
AND THIS IS MY WORK.

THIS IS MY LIFE...

Simon Logan is the author of the underground hit *I-O*, a collection of short stories published by *Prime Books* in 2002 which introduced his style of *industrial* fiction to the world and was met with tremendous success. He has had many short stories featured in various published or soon-to-be published anthologies and had five of his stories highlighted for Honourable Mentions in the latest *Year's Best Fantasy & Horror*, edited by Ellen Datlow. As well as writing industrial fiction Logan also created the style of *fetishcore* fiction as a way of encapsulating the worlds created by fetish artists such as Lee Higgs, Tsubasa, Marco Romano and others in the form of literature. You can find out everything you need to know about him at his website **www.coldandalone.com**.

THE VIRUS HAS ARRIVED

GO INFECT YOURSELF

did. She had no idea what would happen next but what she was certain of was that she wasn't going to lie down and take it.

"The Felidae are going to get fucked over worse than they ever have before," she told him, brushing herself and standing up. "So are you ready, Remy? We've got a lot of work to do."

It seemed like there was never a break and perhaps there never was, never would be. This was life, this was what it was. Battles just filled the time, it was the war that reigned supreme.

But if that was how it was, then so be it.

It was all they had ever known and it was what they were best at.

"Ready Miss," the Digital Cripple said, struggling to stand up.

"Good," the Queen said, smiling ever so slightly. "Now lets break these fuckers off some."

SIXTEEN

So they were outside once more, away from the blood and corpses, in the cool night air and staring out at the horizon. Fires raged in the shells of unfinished skyscrapers, explosives detonated and battle cries sounded. From somewhere near by hip hop music blasted from loudspeakers and car tyres screeched. A shotgun blast.

The hangar was smouldering, leaking thin puffs of dark smoke into the air.

"How are you feeling now?"

"Better," Remy said. His head was swollen with blood but the veins had gone down. He raised the makeshift limb the Hi-Fi Queen had constructed for him, welding a length of piping to his elbow joint and finishing it with an iron slate to act as a foot/hand. "I don't know how long this will last me though."

"Don't worry," the Queen replied. A delicate sulphur-tinged wind blew across her face and the dried blood that caked it. "I've already scheduled a meeting with Whaley. It's time to go for something more aggressive, take a more guerrilla approach to this shit. I figure we keep it lean, just you and me and a few select others, strike hard and fast in key places. I want to hook up with one of the engineering crews, the Split Circuits or NiCads, most likely."

"And the Felidae?"

There was the giant TV screen, glowing against the darkness. It broadcast an entirely new menace now, one thick with creeping shapes and jagged static edges, one that was somehow reflected upon the heavens. Chances are nobody could see what lay within but the Queen

she lived. She wiped blood from her face, drew in a deep breath, and surveyed the theatre. The entire place was lit only by a pale magical glow from the luminous circuit diagrams and tag art that covered the walls and the fire that was spreading across the dead screen. There must have been almost one hundred and fifty headless bodies behind her, another twenty or so intact but lifeless.

"Remy?"

Still ready for another attack, the Queen went to the Digital Cripple and pulled him upright. She opened his eyelids, slapped him twice.

"Miss…?"

"Can you walk?"

"I can barely … barely …"

"It's okay. I'll carry you."

She slipped a slimy arm around his neck, another around his waist.

"Is it over?" Remy asked blearily.

The Hi-Fi Queen let out a little laugh. The theatre was the site of a Bosnian massacre, the place of a serial killer's dream.

"Remy – it's only just started."

And he fell to the ground hard, metal crunching onto the bare concrete. The Queen hurried to him but he was already out cold and she could see the map of angry veins criss-crossing his shaven head. They pulsed in time with the ever-quickening beat of the TV screen.

Another wave, this time strong enough to unbalance her, and another Felidae slumped in their chair.

She reached down and released a couple of catches on Remy's pneumatic limb, detaching it from his body, then hurried back up the steps. In a frenzy she dynamited six, seven, eight Felidae with single, sharp blasts from Remy's dislocated arm and she could feel another wave building and how many had already made it through, what would that mean, just keep going, another Felidae, another, blood and cartilage spraying the air, the shrieking laughed coming from the screen stronger than ever. She worked quickly, efficiently, beheading creature after creature, often standing next to another one as it slumped under the wake of an energy pulse.

There were only a few left now, still staring aimlessly at the screen before them, bereft of thought, of anything.

Her arms ached, she choked on blood. Remy's arm was like a Celtic knot.

And still she continued because she had no idea what would happen now.

One by one, heads mangled and broken.

The Queen lashed out at the final creature and at the same time a further wave swept across her, now strong enough to knock her from her feet and into the slumped creatures beside her. She turned in time to see the static push and mould the screen outwards, something reaching through.

It spoke, the static spoke, but the language was beyond her.

The screen returned to its original shape, the crackling quieting to nothing.

The static flared once, twice, and a gathering of small flames appeared in one corner, moving upwards and across.

Chest heaving, exhausted, the Hi-Fi Queen rose to her feet as she had so many times before and would continue to do for as long as chair's arm until it broke free of its mooring. The end was splinters of sharp, twisted metal.

"Miss…?"

The Hi-Fi Queen lifted the makeshift weapon above her head and struck down on one of the gathered creatures, slamming the metal pieces into and through its skull. She tugged the weapon free, spraying weak blood that seemed to sparkle with energy and then slammed it down again. What was left of the creature was like a wet rose.

"Kill them, Remy. We have to kill them all before they … before they go."

Remy was about to ask where but stopped when another crackle ran across the screen. "Yes Miss."

And so began the wholesale slaughter of the zombie-like Felidae moving from one to the next, collapsing skull after skull, blood spraying, brain matter trickling like royal jelly across the shoulders and backs of the murdered. The TV screen hum deepened, widened, shook the building in a shingle blast of energy and another creature fell limp, another one crossed over.

"Shit, move it, Remy, move it."

Head shattering beneath the Digital Cripple's deviant limb-weapon, he tugged on it and pulled the creature it was embedded in free of its seat, into the growing pools of bodily fluids.

Something within the static shrieked and a visible ripple ran across the surface of the screen as if it were a mere skin which was being pressed against.

The Hi-Fi Queen wiped blood from her face, clotting her hair with it, raised the chair arm once more and roundhoused another creature with it. Bodies slumped, bodies slumped.

Another charge ran through the theatre, dragging one of the creatures into the static to join with its brethren and what sounded like laughter, filtered and refiltered through the grain of transmission, echoed throughout.

"Miss … I'm … tired …." Remy was slumped against a wall, his brow thick with sweat, his distorted limb now even more misshapen and covered with little clumps of Felidae corpse. "My head …"

Nothing.

Still tensed, she moved away slightly from the dead Felidae, watching them carefully, her breathing coming in thick knots.

"I'm sorry Miss, I'm sorry, I'm…."

The Queen tentatively descended a couple of steps, enough to get in front of the Felidae she had just attacked. The creature remained upright as if nothing had happened, the syringe erect in his neck. Eyes open and wide, reflecting the blue glow of the screen.

And next to him, another Felidae with those unmoving, open eyes. And next to him, and next to him.

The whole theatre, full of them.

"What's wrong with them?" Remy asked, now recovered. "Are they dead?"

"No. They're still breathing."

Another wave of electricity washed across them and the giant screen crackled greedily. Shapes moved within it.

TV beckoned.

"They're doing it," the Queen said. "They're actually *doing* it."

"Look," Remy said, pointing further down the rows. A line of six or seven Felidae were slumped in their seats, their heads lolling to one side. The Queen pressed past him to the bottom of the theatre, moving slowly and carefully as if the Felidae would break from their trance at any moment.

She turned and was greeted with an audience of zombie-like Felidae, their slit-eyes glowing with the energy that the complex they had built was focussing into them and for a moment it seemed like they were all reflecting that energy straight at her.

Another blast of electricity almost knocked her over, sweeping out from the screen like a pulse with a visible wave moving up across the TV-numb Felidae. All were still except one on the end of the row, whose head suddenly went limp, its body slumping in the chair. Behind her, the screen fizzed and the Queen turned to see a new shape moving within the static.

"Shit."

She pushed aside one of the slumped Felidae and tugged at the had been newly constructed for before the hangar had been nothing but an empty shell that they had used for storage while the complex was being finished. The markings were precise and infinite.

"What do they mean?" the Queen asked, tracing them with her fingers. They were more than tag, more than marketing boasts and custom-designed straplines.

"Circuit diagrams," Remy told her. "This whole place is a giant conduit."

"A conduit to television."

"So it would seem."

The sound they had first heard while underground was stronger now, emanating, it seemed, through the newly-constructed walls or perhaps *from* the walls as if the sketched circuits actually did carry electricity along their lengths. Like chanting, like a heartbeat.

They followed the passageway to its end, a doorway that looked onto a huge chamber that looked like …

"A cinema," the Queen said.

Rows and rows of seats descended before their eyes and directly opposite an immense television screen that flickered with raw static and menace. Blurred images swirled within the static, glimpse of creatures and events.

When she saw a head move and suddenly realised that the seats were filled with an audience, she jumped back from the doorway, pulling more syringes from her garter belt.

"They're here", she said. "All of them."

"What are they doing?"

She paused. "Watching."

"Watching?"

"Watching."

Remy moved past her to get a better look but he caught his disfigured limb on the door jamb and stumbled forwards, clattering into the back of the first row of seats and onto the occupant. The Queen quickly jumped at the figure, slamming the syringe into his neck once, twice, then pushing Remy back, ready for the return attacks that she knew would come.

As if in response to the unease in her voice, the giant TV screen on the horizon flickered once, twice and a wave of electricity washed over them. The two stuck to the side of the hangar as they made their way around, careful not to be caught off-guard by any lingering assaults but by the time they reached the generator it truly did seem certain that the Felidae had bigger concerns than territory. At least, not physical territory.

The Hi-Fi Queen opened a hatch by the thrumming machine, and peered into the darkness before starting her descent. "Can you make it?" she called up to Remy when she reached the bottom.

The man struggled with his damaged crutch but was by now proficient enough in their usage to lower himself carefully rung by rung into the dark, wet passageway. Weak strip lighting lit the way for around fifty metres, far enough to get under the heart of the hangar.

"This could be a trap," Remy pointed out.

"It could be. But why let us get this far before trying anything? Those Felidae back at the main building were just leftovers, probably grunts that were deceived into thinking they were some sort of special guards for a complex the gang doesn't care if they lose. They must all be in here."

"Why?" Remy asked, then stopped when he realised he already knew the answer.

The corridor fell into darkness at around about the same time the sounds became apparent – a low, scratchy murmur like recorded breathing. Another set of steps led up to another hatch and the Hi-Fi Queen opened it without pause. She just wanted this over and done with now.

"Shit."

"What? Miss? What do you see?"

Her legs vanished through the gap and Remy hurried after her though he found that climbing the steps was infinitely more difficult than coming down them. When he made it up into the passageway he saw what she had seen.

Inscribed on the walls, ceiling and floor were luminous diagrams annotated with hieroglyphics and unnameable symbols. The passage

FIFTEEN

Every entrance to the hangar was sealed with thick gobs of a dull grey solder that held heavy iron plates across the doorways, leaving the structure as a completely faceless brick of concrete. Tag art covered it up to a height of around 20 metres, aggressive threats and assertions of Felidae power that looked so uneven in places that it must have been done by the Felidae themselves rather than any hired crew.

The whole building glowed with menace and blue-green light.

"How's that leg? Or … arm…" the Queen asked, running a hand across the defaced concrete.

"Awkward," the Digital Cripple replied. He held up the crutch-arm he had mangled in the jump from the overhead corridor, turning it in the voodoo light. "But that's nothing compared to the pain in my head."

"The signals?"

"I've never experienced anything like it."

The Hi-Fi Queen looked around at the bland landscape of the landing strip and the unfinished areas beyond. Wrecked cars were piled up near the perimeter fencing, small fires glowing within their rusting carcasses. There were battles taking place beyond the fencing but within it … nothing.

"What do we do?" Remy asked.

"There's an access tunnel around the back by the generator that allows engineering access to the landing strip lights. I've got a horrible feeling that they don't care if we're coming or not but there's only one way to find out."

crackling energy emanating from the hangar. There was still far too much silence for her liking. She stepped out into the midnight air and began to shimmy down the cabling then once on the ground looked up to the Digital Cripple expectantly.

"I have the distinct feeling of impending doom, Miss. I don't think I'm going to make it through the night," he called down to her as he edged towards the opening, crutches banging awkwardly against the rough metal edges of the unfinished passageway.

He didn't hear the Queen's answer because of the noise of air rushing past him after he jumped closely followed by the sound of his own screaming.

the ground in time for Remy to stamp on their heads with a hiss of steam ejaculating from his hip joint. The third creature had retreated back a few paces and was readying itself for another blast of flame, still struggling with the trigger because of its unfeasibly long nails when the Hi-Fi Queen grabbed it by the hair and bit into its neck then shoved a needle into its stomach and gave it a complete dose of her infection. As it fell to the ground, she snatched at the flame thrower and pulled it free.

"Man, they stink," she said, leaning over the sorry creatures.

"It's not them," Remy explained. "It's in the air. I think it's the broadcasts."

"It smells like shit."

Remy nodded in pneumatic agreement. Ahead of them a long corridor stretched out like a dislocated rib over the runway. Most of the glass was missing from the windows and thick, steamy air clotted their lungs. They walked along the corridor cautiously, ready for any further attacks but it was obvious the Felidae's attention lay elsewhere and that was bad news. In the distance they could see the giant TV screen that for now was filled with blurred imagery and pixellated chaos. For now.

"This leads straight to the hangar, right?" the Queen asked.

"It did when the Motherboard was ours. The construction wasn't finished though."

And as they soon saw, the Felidae hadn't bothered to complete the corridor for at the very end there was not a doorway but an open space fragmented by struts of skeletal framework and a thirty foot drop to the solid concrete runway below. The Queen and Remy looked down and saw that a piece of thick coaxial cabling had been tied around one of the exposed rods and left to hang towards the ground.

"Can you make it?" the Queen asked and it seemed to take Remy a moment to realise his new-found difficulty with his crutches.

"Looks like I'll have to," he said and nodded towards the immense bulk of the hangar. "It's ... *glowing*. Miss – you don't think they're actually close enough to make it do you? To actually televise themselves?"

The Queen didn't answer, growing increasingly nervous at the emained hidden.

Or otherwise occupied.

"This way. Shit, it's getting stronger."

She chased after Remy as he charged pneumatically towards the ertiary wing of departure lounges. With each step, memories of the place infected her, swollen particles in her bloodstream that felt as if hey would finalise themselves as clots in her dizzied mind. All the iights she had wandered the empty halls as the others formed plans in he makeshift war rooms; the dead they had dragged back from a riot aid out side by side in the First Aid centre.

They swung down a carpeted ramp and out into concrete :orridors, unfinished and pitch black in places.

"It's definitely this way," Remy told her. "Towards the hangar. 5hit, Miss, this is big. Perhaps we should wait until we have more .. upport?"

"From whom, Remy? Most of them are too busy picking off pieces of *our* land or more concerned with their own battles."

"But if they knew …"

"If they knew the Felidae were fucking with TV we'd have a 1elluva lot more trouble on our hands than we already do".

"Oh I think you've got plenty already," a voice said a split second before a storm of fire blasted out of the darkness of one of the corridors.

The Hi-Fi Queen rolled away instinctively, pulling Remy with 1er but he stumbled against the wall as he fell and there was the sound of metal tearing, steam hissing and he was screaming as he hit the ground And the Felidae, three of them, one with a small flamethrower and the others with knives emerged from the orange glow of the passageway with its inner lining on fire, turning the weapons on the Queen as she ducked out of the way again, grabbing Remy's crutch as she went then :urning, twisting before they could re-aim and shoving the crutch upwards in one lightning movement into the creature's face, splitting its :heek.

Within the echo of its cry she rolled forwards, pulling the crutch with her and toppling the creature before slicing it horizontally and :hrough the thighs of its brother, another swing and they both fell to

FOURTEEN

If you were to wander into the city's deviant streets, lie with the festering souls that inhabited it, reach into their soft skulls and feel their dreams with the tips of your finger, you would see everything described in the electron glow of a vacuum tube, filtered and divided into 525 interlaced lines. You would see that when they pictured power it was not in the air but on TV and when they pictured a god they were not in the heavens but on the last channel on the dial, embracing the static as the cosmos embraces every star, every piece of debris.

There was no greater dream than to exert yourself on television.

"No wonder they lost the territory so quickly," the Hi-Fi Queen said as she followed Remy, who continued to follow the scent of the electricity through the unfinished booking-in area, through a baggage chute then out into the loading hangar and back into the booking-in area again. "They weren't even *trying* to hold onto it – that didn't matter. What mattered was this place."

She tapped a sign on a wall which half-fulfilled its purpose as a map. The names of arrival and departure gates, of the lost property section and of cafés and shops, were all displayed in neat white writing but hung in mid-air without any accompanying directions, thereby transformed into ethereal deities – Bloc 9, Bloc 10, Bistro and Lst. Propty.

"We have to find them."

As Remy felt his way through the channels of ghost static that ribboned through the vast empty corridors, the Hi-Fi Queen looked up at a CCTV camera that followed her as she moved. The Felidae knew they were there, would know *exactly* where they were and yet they with your crutches."

Remy nodded unquestioningly, leaned back and raised one crutch-arm up and then drove it into the bulkhead, tearing through the metal. A shower of sparks burst out like wasps that had been disturbed, little bolts of power streaking through them.

She waved her hands to clear the smoke that issued from the hole and stared in at the massive coil of dozens of wires wrapped around each other that lay within. "What. The. Fuck."

Remy stepped closer, struggling with just one crutch, his renegade joints gasping with the strain. The cables were as thick as his fist and translucent, thousands of micro-fibre wires visible within, wires that seemed to move like worms with the energy they carried.

"What's going *on* here?" the Hi-Fi Queen asked.

"It can't be. This can't be."

There was enough give on the cables for Remy to pull one out of the bundle and examine it more closely. He leaned forward, bit down on the plastic and held it tight between his teeth as the muscles in his face and neck shuddered, then suddenly leapt backwards from it, stumbling away and falling to the ground.

He stared back up at the Hi-Fi Queen in shock, spat a small ribbon of smoke from his mouth. "That's TV cabling."

And everything suddenly became so much worse.

It edged forward, preparing to leap at her and the Hi-Fi Queen readied herself – then watched as it fell onto the plastic-layered floor.

"That was easier than I thought it would be," Remy said, standing where the cat-creature had been moments before, the spiked end of his crutch sheathed in the Felidae's blood from where he had shoved it into its back.

"If slightly messier." The Hi-Fi Queen remained alert, ready for more Felidae to appear having been summoned by the death-screech of their fellow pride member but no one appeared. "Something's wrong. This isn't right."

"Miss?" Remy asked, wiping the ends of his crutch with a loose piece of bandage that hung from his waist.

He watched as the woman walked across to the nearest wall, more a bulkhead, and pressed her ear against it. She jumped back suddenly, clutching the side of her face.

"Jesus!"

Gingerly she moved her hand closer to the metal plating, watched the tiny hairs on her arms stand up. "Remy what are you getting?"

"Nothing, Miss. Why?"

"Nothing at all?"

He shook his head.

"Remy, we're at the Felidae's final stronghold – and you're getting *nothing*?"

He considered this for a moment, closed his eyes to the room, then opened them again. "Interference. Massive interference."

"But from what? The only power source that was built before we claimed this place was an old generator that could manage barely six or seven rooms."

"They must be tapping in somewhere, leeching it from the electrical fields."

"What for? What could they possibly gain from powering this place up? There's nothing of value to them here."

The Digital Cripple shrugged. "I guess there must be something."

"I guess there must. Do me a favour, blast a hole right there

THIRTEEN

Without a second thought the Hi-Fi Queen smashed through the window and grabbed at the Felidae but it was too fast, spinning away from her fist and sprinting off down the long, wide corridor of the terminal and there was something different about the way it moved …

She chased after it, Remy hissing and pumping away on limbs he was growing more adept at moving on with each hour that passed, along the soft carpeted terminal passageway, through a doorway and into the baggage handling room. The Felidae was perched atop the unmoving conveyor belt, its clawed hands wrapped around the metal rim of the device. Overhead strip-lights flickered in random patches in the ceiling.

They were changing. Some sort of evolutionary acceleration was taking place that went far beyond anything even Whaley's makeover team would have been capable, never mind the third-rate agency the Felidae had been forced to use.

Remy moved around the outside of the room, attempting to get on the other side of the Felidae but the creature turned itself to keep an eye on both of them. The Hi-Fi Queen plucked a needle from the belt on her thigh and yielded it like a dart, wary of every movement that came from the darkness. The Felidae held its hand out and unsheathed its claws fully, each one glinting in the starlight that filtered in.

"I'm not sure exactly what's going on with you guys but I'm guessing that your little biological additions there still aren't going to be enough to beat me at a game of quick draw."

The Felidae hiss-smiled. "You think so?"

The Chevy drew closer and closer to the main terminal in utter silence, the satellite dishes still, the runway lights dead. The Phenyl Barbiedoll could see the Felidaes' cosmic eyes glittering in the darkened windows, could sense them moving around in the subterranean passages.

This wasn't going to be easy.

"Hang on," the Phenyl Barbiedoll said as they stepped out of the Chevy and approached the great windows of the terminal. She picked up a can of spray paint then leaned forward so that her hair hung cleanly away from her face then sprayed what was left over the blonde strands Whaley had designed for her.

"We can hardly go creeping around with hair so platinum you can almost see your reflection in it," she said, finishing off the underside. "How's that?"

The Digital Cripple moved pneumatically towards her, his machine parts filling the dark air with little puffs of steam. "She's back, Miss," he said somewhat dreamily. "I knew she'd return."

The Phenyl Barbiedoll stared quizzically back at him, dropped the spraypaint to the ground. "Who's back?"

Remy motioned with a piston arm to one of the plates of glass and the reflection that was described within it. "The Hi-Fi Queen is back."

And he was right. Piece by piece the Phenyl Barbiedoll had been discarded and its former incarnation had been returned.

The Hi-Fi Queen stared at herself – at the industrial boots, the ragged, uneven clothing, the engine oil and the spillage of pitch black hair around her shoulders. The sight of her old self was like a ghost of both past and future, a premonition of inevitability, and filled her with confidence as if it were a drug.

She glanced over her shoulder at Remy when she turned back again it was no longer her own image that presented itself to her in the reflection but that of a Felidae, baring its rotten fangs at her through the glass.

elbows, then took a moment to draw in the grand view of her logo glowing brightly across the empty lot as if it were a shrine to her own return to magnificence. And directly in front of them, one of the Mansons hung from the fencing, arms and legs spread by tight bonds of coaxial wire, internal organs pinned to his outer body in the shape of an Ankh. It was revenge for what they had done to the captured Felidae, yes, but more so a warning.

And a terribly unoriginal one at that.

The Phenyl Barbiedoll sat back in the Chevy and steered it through one of many gaps that had been torn in the fencing, alert and ready for an attack to pour out of the darkness. Tiny enzymes of memory flared within her as she drove over the heart of her old territory, now seemingly all that was *left* of her old territory.

And at the back of the area was the airport that had been aborted mid-construction, a foetus that had been abandoned while still half-formed and taken into the Hi-Fi Queen's own womb to complete its maturation. It had been anointed the Motherboard, this concoction of great concrete edifices capped by shining masts and satellite dishes, linked by underground tunnels and glass walkways that often led nowhere, like arteries attempting to feed nutrients to organs that didn't exist.

"Do you feel that?" Remy asked, tilting his head to one side.

"What?"

He seemed to concentrate on something for a few moments, then shrugged, shook his head. "Nothing. Probably nothing."

They pulled onto the unfinished runway strip that bled from the main building, driving past numerous bodies, both Felidae and Mansons, and the Phenyl Barbiedoll smiled inwardly. Her entire body was alert, ready for the kind of cowardly attack that had caught her out previously.

A firework exploded overhead, assuming the shape of an ankh for a few moments before dispersing into an atomic shower of bright sparks. A useless show of bravado.

Things remained quiet as the Chevy rolled across the runway that surrounded the Motherboard and they quickly realised that the Felidae weren't going to make it easy by showing themselves in the open.

TWELVE

By the time they reached the barbed wire fences that lined the edges of Lithium Valley it was getting dark. Jinx and his crew were working the concrete pillars that had been erected on some spare land just inside the fencing to provide the framework of a skyscraper that never came along, standing like thick grey trees in the wilderness. The tag artists had switched to luminous paint that made full use of the radioactive air in the Valley, etching the Phenyl Barbiedoll's logo everywhere they could.

In the distance were the sounds of battle and framed against a purple sky the extensive structure that had once been an outpost of the late Hi-Fi Queen's digital army. The suicidal addicts that inhabited Lithium Valley stumbled around like zombies, nothing but terrified insect-shadows that would pose no threat.

"They know who we are, mistress. Or who we were," Remy said as ammunitions lit up the sky like fireworks, their reflections scampering across the rusted, battered hood of the Chevy. She was working beneath it, repairing the damage of point-blank shotgun blasts and her hyper-aggressive driving. "And they know that we're coming."

"Good."

"Their broadcast crew seems to have stopped pumping out propaganda, I'm guessing because they ran out of funds. They've pulled back all their members, consolidated them in the Valley. They know we're heading for the Motherboard."

"Which means they know it's just a matter of time."

She stood up from the humming engine, having peeled off the velvet gloves and replaced them with a covering of motor oil up to her

ELEVEN

The Chevy drifted across the hot concrete, kicking up chalk dust on either side as it went, suddenly skidding to a halt before they had reached the main thoroughfare. The almost literal half-man that was what was left of the Felidae coughed weakly a few yards ahead on one side, wearily looking up through the dust clouds and whining pathetically as the Phenyl Barbiedoll climbed out of the Chevy and came towards him.

He had made only a vague start on the pleading that he was about to commence when she opened her mouth, pushed a finger to the back of her throat, then began to vomit onto him. The semi-digested chunks of the other Felidae poured over him, lubed by a liberal amount of stomach acid and several bottles worth of the mineral water she had been plied with back at the agency. Once done, she spat the remaining mulch from her mouth then returned to the Chevy, leaving the Felidae somewhat startled and glistening.

She wiped her mouth once again with one gloved forearm. "Stings," she said.

"Miss? Are you ... feeling alright?"

She politely let out a little gas, nodding. "I just have to watch myself," she told him, leaving the Felidae behind, dripping and more than a little stunned. "Meat like that will go straight to my thighs."

Remy raised an eyebrow. Seems like everything could be marketed after all.

had been done to the car's inner workings.

"What about the canal? The scavengers are already moving in."

"I see them. But we've got more important things to do than fend off Man-Dogs and Lobotomy Blondes from periphery land. We might as well skip any bullshit and get straight to the heart of the territory. They *do* still have the Motherboard don't they? Tell me they have the Motherboard."

"For now," Remy told her, his joints hissing as he leaned back in the seat. "But who knows how much longer they'll be able to hold onto it?"

"Then that's where we're heading. Hold on tight, Remy."

"Yes, Miss. Oh, and – Miss?"

"What?"

"You've got a little bit of meat .. just on your ..."

"Where? I can't ..." She tongued her teeth in the Chevy's mirror.

"No .. just .. up .. that's ... just ...."

"Here? I ... oh .. got it. Did that get it?"

"Yes, Miss. That got it."

pick clean what the Felidae had abandoned. The Rivetheads, the Digital Plasma Collective and Bikini Kill were all amongst those approaching cautiously through the rubble and car wrecks.

When the Phenyl Barbiedoll had finished, she dumped the final corpse and stalked back over to the car. Her arms and face were smeared in clotted blood and she had torn the bottom half of her dress off to make the feast easier, exposing the needle-clad thigh that carried another seven doses of her embryonic reptile infection. She wiped her face as she climbed back into the Chevy, sighing just as the car creaked.

Remy waited a few moments then said, "Are you still allowed … I mean … is it in your contracted image…?"

She licked her lips, groaned somewhat orgasmically. "I guess some pieces of me just can't be marketed," she pondered, shrugging. "He's doing not half bad, isn't he?"

She nodded over towards the humanoid slug currently about half a mile away towards the other side of the concrete plains. A trail of blood that grew wetter the closer it got to him snaked behind him with puddles where he had passed out or found himself unable to continue until he had heard the wet, ripping sounds of the Phenyl Barbiedoll helping herself to the rest of his crew.

"I guess. But he'll never make it. We'll be there long before him."

"Of course. But you have to send one of their own back to warn the others. It increases tension – standard self-promotion technique. Besides, these fuckers aren't going to be any sort of problem for us, crew or no crew. There's no rush."

"Perhaps – but only if it's them we have to fight to get the territory back. There are skirmishes breaking out all over the place. They may just be small bites that are being taken but …"

His words trailed off somewhat as the image of his mistress sucking on a set of lower intestines like they were spaghetti flickered through his mind.

"You're right," she said, relieving him of the need to finish the sentence – and the flashback. She turned the key and revved the engine to life, dispelling the Digital Cripple's fears that some serious damage

TEN

A little later, the Digital Cripple sat in the back of the Chevy, the side door where he had previously been now missing, having been so shot up that it made more sense just to rip it free. He squirmed uncomfortably as the Phenyl Barbiedoll finished plucking pieces of meat away from the dead Felidae. She hadn't touched any of the dead Cranials, her consumption restricted to that of her enemies and the Cranials were only her enemies by proxy. If anything she would be grateful to them for providing one of many distractions that would make her return to domination as swift and painless as she hoped.

He stared blankly at a Cranial corpse lying slumped against a small pile of cigarettes from an ashtray that had been emptied there. It was quite incredible what a shotgun blast to the head could do to a person – even more incredible that the Cranials could function at all with half-exploded eyeballs and skulls that were folded back on themselves and glistened with brain matter.

Framed against the sky was one of the handful of gigantic LCD screens that transmitted the realm of those that had ascended the city's dirty, infested streets and into TV. That was the ultimate, that was Nirvana, for once you were TV that was the only place you existed. The trivialities of gang warfare were shed in front of the glaring light of cathode ray magnificence and you became something more.

Bur for now their energies had to be focused on their current situation. He tuned in and out of the various radio broadcasts he managed to receive so knew before he first spotted them on the industrial horizon that small packs of scavengers were moving in on the area to

een aware of the rumours about what she did to her kills in her past
ncarnation. The stronger and more evil the enemy is said to be, the
reater the defeat for those who achieve it – that idea went even further
ack than Ancient Egypt. Of course he'd know.

He groaned dreamily as his fears were confirmed for him – for
nce what the airwaves said wasn't a lie. The Barbiedoll leaned down
nd tore a chunk of flesh away from the dead girl, stuffing it into her
nouth with both stained hands – and another, and another. Then the
elidae made a sound somewhat like a squeal and began dragging himself
way with more gusto than he even would have thought possible.

discarded crates, watching him through the cracks. The Felidae hissed in anger, knew there was nowhere to go. "Out you come. Come on now."

And suddenly he broke his cover and in that moment he was dead, before the Phenyl Barbiedoll had whipped the shotgun into her hands, before she had cocked it, before she had fired two shells straight into him. He was dead because she wished him so and even after six comatose months she had more power and grace than the reincarnated cat-spirits would ever hope to steal.

He dropped to the ground in a wet heap, slit eyes blazing as she stood over him and brought the barrel down to bear on his drawn face. A moment passed and then his eyes widened.

"That's it. You recognise me now? Do you know who I am, little kitty?"

And it was easier to catch the resemblance now, despite Whaley and his teams' efforts. Her dress was torn along its slit, her thighs and knees smeared in oil and concrete dust, her hair crumpled and hanging in strands instead of the neat crop it had been in. That, and the boots and shotgun made sure the Felidae recognised the Hi-Fi Queen.

"Oh shit," he spluttered, pulling himself away from her on a pair of damaged legs. "There's going to be trouble isn't there?"

"There is," the Phenyl Barbiedoll said calmly. "So go tell them." The Felidae glanced at the weapon, wary that it was still loaded.

"I amn't going to shoot you. Well .. not again. I'm going to give you a head start. We've got the Chevy, you've got ..." she looked at his bloodied, partially severed legs, ".. those. Not exactly fair but then again neither was cowardly thieving my territory, right?"

The Felidae nodded, blood bubbles emerging involuntarily from his mouth.

"Go on then, little kitty, run home."

He began to pull himself away, dragging himself along the stinking puddles as best he could. "I ... can't ..."

The Phenyl Barbiedoll smiled once, dropped her weapon, then crossed to one of the cat warrior's dead comrades. She bent down beside the woman, glanced back at the sole survivor. She knew he would have as the Phenyl Barbiedoll skidded over her, a couple of Cranials shuddering across the car's elongated, wide hood long enough for her to get a clear view of their radically distorted heads before they collided with the windscreen and slid off.

She threw the vehicle around, bringing it to a halt and grabbing one of the dead Cranial's weapons. Thankfully they were a better shot than they had been when they had turned their respective guns on themselves to get membership into the gang – a smattering of murdered Felidae lay amongst the marshy waters and junk. The Phenyl Barbiedoll rose from behind the shattered windscreen, cocking the shotgun and blowing away one of the Felidae, which hissed as he hit the ground sans one-third of his torso. Buckshot ricocheted off of the Chevy next to the Digital Cripple, huddled behind the door. The airwaves were alive with static above them as the gangs jammed and re-jammed each others signals and cut into their advertising blocks.

The Phenyl Barbiedoll fired again, again, all the old ways flooding back to her as bodies fell all around her. She threw the shotgun at the ground when it was spent, leaping out of the car in a way she would never have attempted should she have still had her prescribed heels on. A shot whizzed past her head as she bent down to pick up a fresh weapon, spinning backwards towards the car then under it. She smiled to herself in the oily darkness. This was going to be easier than she had feared.

She waited a few moments, listening to the sounds of the gang members escaping, knowing that their petty skirmish had been rumbled by a far superior fighter, then rolling out from under and blasting the shotgun.

Within a minute there was only one Felidae left that hadn't either gotten away or been slaughtered. The Cranials were long gone, cowards as they were, save for the dead amongst them (a difficult state to be certain of considering the condition their heads were in while alive). She was cautious as she rounded on the remaining cat-warrior, hunched as he was behind two oil drums so littered with gunshots that they more resembled winter trees. She was aware of everything around her, of all the bodies and all the weapons.

"C'mon, little puss," she teased, easing herself behind some

NINE

She read the signals as they drove, past burnt-out wrecks and collapsed garages, past small fights and groups of people huddled around oil drum fires. Everyone was moving in on the Felidae – even low-key players like the Cranials were taking small chunks where they could.

"The Cranials are the failed shotgun suicides, right?" she asked, revving the engine.

Remy nodded.

"So how desperate for territory to you have to be to agree to a dire hook like that?"

Remy shrugged.

"Shit. And these are the assholes taking *my* land?"

She drew the Chevy up alongside the channel where the canal started. Down below, in the sludgy water that was all that was left of the artificial stream that once ran through, there was a body. A few hundred yards along the canal the skirmish was still going on, the crack of double-barrel shotguns filling the air.

"Ready, Remy?"

The Digital Cripple nodded.

She kicked the car into high gear and threw it over the lip of the canal and towards the fighters, the suspension bucking them as one of the Felidae was thrown backwards by a gunshot that left his right leg standing free of the rest of him, swinging around, swerving as the gangs finally registered her an instant before she ploughed through a scrapping group of them.

A Felidae fell beneath the Chevy's wheels, twisting and shrieking

"And then?"

"Seizures? Vomiting? Mild psychotic episodes? I'm not quite sure. I never got a chance to test the effects fully."

"Then death?"

She shrugged. "I guess."

EIGHT

"So what did you get?" she asked as the Chevy burned its way through the grey desert dust. They were heading south towards the canal district leaving the newly energised Mansons to go down Lithium Valley.

"Not much," Remy told her, joints hissing as he tried to get comfy in the back seat. "There was a little inference, the airwaves are pretty jammed up right now. The Felidae are losing territory fast. It sounded like the Cranials but I couldn't be sure."

"The Cranials? They've moved this far down?"

"Only into Felidae territory, apparently."

"Shit. We have to move fast before the bastards lose it all."

She swung a right across a parking lot filled only with rows of burned-out vandalised vehicles and construction supplies from unfinished buildings then came to a sudden halt. Got out the car.

"Miss?" Remy asked, not sure whether to follow or not.

She looked around amongst the construction trash, then finally pulled something out. A pair of old hobnailed boots. She slipped them onto her feet, tearing the cocktail dress slightly as she pulled it out of the way. She sighed with relief then got back into the car, started off again.

"Miss? What did you give them? The Mansons?" Remy asked her some way down the road.

"Just what I said. A cocktail of hyper-vitamins plus a little extra."

A pause. "How long have they got?"

She smiled to herself. "Given their current state I had to dilute the doses slightly but enough time for them to cause some havoc with the Felidae."

He sighed as she injected him, too weak to struggle, and the chemicals moved visibly up her crooked veins.

"Ohhhh … fffuuuuuuccckk .."

The others stepped back as he slid onto his knees, shaking, utterly defenceless in their deteriorated state. Then halted where they were when he looked up at them, smiling broadly.

"That's *gooood…*"

"Here's the deal – I help you get yourselves healthy again and in return you help the Digital Cripple and I to track down and kill the rest of these motherfuckers."

They still regarded her warily but as the male Manson rolled onto his back, still smiling, his skin warming before their very eyes, another of their number held out her arm. The Phenyl Barbiedoll sank the needle in and injected another fifth of the syringe's content in.

"What is it?" another asked, stepping forwards.

"A cocktail of hyper-vitamins, mostly, plus a few extras. Enough to get you back into a position to fight for yourselves again and get out of this fucking dump."

She dropped a couple more needles onto the platform and left them to scramble amongst themselves for the drug. Things were going perfectly.

"Miss …" Remy said, his head twitching spastically.

"The only caveat is that you don't *touch* any of the Felidae's territory yourselves."

The Mansons were too busy feeling the rush of hyper-vitamins and codeine derivatives to pay much attention to her.

"Miss …" Remy repeated, face creasing as he listened to his internal radio. "There's a skirmish, down by the canal. The Felidae…."

The Phenyl Barbiedoll smiled. "And so it begins."

raise her head but seemed unable.

"I don't think she ..." Remy started, then was silenced when another figure stepped out of the darkness. He was dressed, predictably, entirely in black with shades and a top hat to finish it off.

"We've kept her alive," he said, not coming too close. Another handful of figures, again dressed in black and moving slowly, emerged around him. "We wouldn't kill her. We just ... need her."

"Are there more?"

"Just her now."

The Phenyl Barbiedoll crossed to the Felidae, pulled her head upright. The slit cat-eyes were dull, seeming to just rest aimlessly in their sockets.

"Do you recognise me?" she asked the woman.

Shock gripped the Felidae as tight as the tomb of one of her long-dead Egyptian masters. There would be no satisfaction there.

"You can take her," the Manson said. When Phenyl turned to face him she saw that they were all propping each other up, as if sharing out the little energy they had left through touch. "Just don't ... *do* anything ..."

The Phenyl Barbiedoll walked across to them, past Remy who shuffled into line behind her. She was conscious of her bare feet, stripping her of a few extra inches of height, but still she loomed over the Manson. "Give me your arm."

One of the female Mansons gripped the one with the top hat with a single shaking hand. "Just take her and go. We don't want any trouble. Please."

"We aren't interested in her – I'd like your help. Now, hold out your arm."

Visibly wary, the man did so, exposing the withered flesh of his forearm and the bulging blue veins. The gathered Mansons breathed audibly at the site and Phenyl wondered how long it might be until they had completely drained the Felidae and started feasting on each other. She raised one of the syringes and placed it on his skin, holding him tight with ease as he tried to pull back.

"What are you doing? Please, we don't ..."

of the steel ribbing that roofed them. Remy thought he saw movements but couldn't be certain.

They continued their climb as they both felt the old buzz of battle begin to come back, suddenly realising that they had little in the way of weapons. The Phenyl Barbiedoll touched the hypodermics that were strapped onto her garter belt but felt little comfort. She wanted one of her old metal bars or razors.

"They were a part of the Leeches at some point," she said as they corned the ramp and moved up into the catwalk. "But there was in-fighting and the Mansons went their own way. Couldn't afford a decent design consultant and ended up getting fucked over."

"How so?"

"They're Mansons, goths. They look great but they're too fucked up to crawl out of …" and she motioned once more to the ceiling, where this time there was definitely movements, "… the darkness. I think most of them were wiped out long ago but I'd heard some had been roosting here before …"

A drop of blood spattered in front of them.

The Phenyl Barbiedoll drew one of the syringes from its sheath as they crept ahead, beneath the landing from which the blood had come. She knew the Mansons wouldn't attack, they were too goddamned weak from trying to stay as emaciated as their consultant deemed necessary to maintain their image, and so they climbed the steps and came up onto the landing. At the end was a concrete wall and nailed onto the wall, spread-eagled, was one of the Felidae. Her hair was falling from her head as her scalp shrunk, her naked form more like a juxtaposition of bones than anything vaguely human, her skin littered with tiny cuts but her giveaway Ankh tattoo was as clearly inscribed upon her stomach as it had ever been.

Her head was hung low enough that she did not realise the Phenyl Barbiedoll and the Digital Cripple were standing before her until Phenyl said, "We're not here to cause you any trouble," but louder than necessary, into thin air.

There was movement in the rafters and from further along the pre-fabbed corridor that led off of the platform. The Felidae tried to interesting."

From a distance the mill looked long abandoned but then what else was an abandoned steel mill meant to look like? It was surrounded by half an acre of concrete slabs with mould lining the cracks between them. There was a large insignia sprayed onto the slabs that led up to the main entrance into the vast crumbling complex, that of an Ankh.

The Phenyl Barbiedoll touched her belly where the tattoo that had defaced her had been lasered away.

"So do we go in?" Remy asked. He'd questioned her once about coming here when they had been told the Felidae had moved on down to Lithium Valley but once was enough, he knew his place was the same as it was before. At her side.

Phenyl smiled once then kicked the Chevy into gear, throwing up a curtain of dust behind them as the wheels spun on the concrete. She worked the heavy steering wheel, dragging the car through a series of railings then down a small slope and into the dark, pipe-infested belly of the mill before hitting the brakes awkwardly. The car swerved one way then the other and finally came to a halt inches from a massive generator.

"Fucking! Heels!" she shouted and leapt from the car, kicking wildly until both shoes came flying off. They scattered into the shadows, the sound vibrating through the cold metal.

And beyond that sound, another.

Remy climbed from the car awkwardly, still adjusting to his new form. His joints hissed pneumatically, suddenly freezing when the Phenyl Barbiedoll motioned to him to be quiet. He listened for a few moments then heard the groans too.

Together they began up a ramp that led to the first floor deck, a metal catwalk running overhead and up into the main parts of the building. "I think they're here," Phenyl said, grinning. Her barefooted movements were silent compared to the Digital Cripple's ragged hybrid ones but he was fast learning how to move more athletically.

"The Felidae?"

She shook her head, displacing a few moussed blonde hairs on one side. "The Mansons," she said and looked upwards to the darkness

SEVEN

"Coming through now," the Digital Cripple said not long after the steel mill had become etched in the horizon like something out of a Giger sketch. He tilted his head to one side. "Yeah, they've got it going on now. I think it's somewhere in the middle of the dial but it's getting a lot of interference from the other broadcasters."

The Phenyl Barbiedoll played with the Chevy's radio tuner, trying to pick up what Remy was having shoved into his scarred cranium but the signal was too weak just yet. The pirate radio crew were, Whaley assured her, one of the better ones around but the battle for the airwaves was growing almost as intense as that between the gangs themselves. Many said that soon the fights would become purely propaganda, information warfare, and that the streets would be empty and silent. But for now it was as it always had been – blood and blade and chemicals and nailbombs. For now the pirates were content with stealing each others bandwidth and jamming their own signals down it, advertising whatever gang's payroll they were on.

Right now, in the city, it didn't matter one iota if you won a fight for turf if there was no advertising to highlight the fact. Of course, not all the information was solid. The broadcast pirates were constantly adding new levels to the complexity of mind games they waged, double-bluffing each other, secretly buying other stations out and in the process crushing any gangs challenging those they already helped out by launching media viruses.

Sometimes it seemed more trouble than it was worth.

"Just keep tracking it – and let me know if you get anything else

Shoot."

"Work Ramo-Tep and the Felidae for me. Mix it up a little with them for me – tag near their tag. Maybe even accidentally get little *too* close and erase them."

Jinx laughed "Shheee-eet. You trying to start somethin' precious?"

"The question is – are *you*?"

"Ha. I ain't willing to risk my crew's necks, or better yet my own, fucking with the rules. There's plenty space for everyone here if y'all just chilled a little. First rule of tag – you don't fuck with other artists' work."

"But some of it is *your* work if like you said you did some tagging for them in the past. Come on," the Phenyl Barbiedoll said. She felt herself slouching slightly against the Chevy, legs parting, the dress slipping away from her thighs and revealing the garter belt. "A favour for me."

Jinx was silent for a moment then began laughing again. "Sheee-et. I think we might be able to swing something for you, lady. But look, these fuckers ain't nothing. They're small fry. They losing shit like they got diarrhoea or somethin'. You want to get somewhere, there're better players to make moves on."

"Maybe so. But I like taking things slow – makes it all the more enjoyable. That okay with you?"

"Mmmm-hmmm," Jinx said, one eyebrow raising. "Whatever you say."

He reached into his rucksack and pulled out a can, popped the top and quickly sprayed the Phenyl Barbiedoll's newly-designed logo on the tyre wall. "That one's for free."

After the deal had been finalised and the tag crew had left the Phenyl Barbiedoll sat back down in the Chevy and breathed out. She looked down at herself, examined one gloved and sparkling hand by the diminishing daylight. "What the fuck just happened back there?"

The Digital Crippled smiled, shrugged. "Miss – it appears that you now have sex appeal."

The Phenyl Barbiedoll frowned, glanced down at the line of blood on her ankle where the heels were digging in. "Goddamnit."

when talking to someone, and suddenly wished she hadn't as the guys leered at her thigh when it was revealed by the dress's slit. She prayed inwardly that she wouldn't stumble on the heels and settled for casually leaning against the Chevy's hood for support just to be safe.

She wanted fear in their eyes – not lust.

"Listen, I know that Whaley deals with Ramo-Tep and the Felidae – your crew ever done any tag for them?"

Jinx looked blank for a few moments, turned to the others behind him, then back to the Phenyl Barbiedoll. "Never heard of the motherfuckers. Which ones they again?"

"The Egyptian cat-spirits. Slit green eyes, lots of gold, feisty little bastards."

"Ahhh, yeah, now you're talking. I'm wit' you now. Yeah we done some shit for them but I think Whaley's got a couple of other crews hanging for them now. They boarders, right?"

"In a previous incarnation."

Jinx was nodding emphatically now. "Know the ones. Used to hang out in the old steel mill. Plenty to grind up there, let me tell you."

At his words the Phenyl Barbiedoll felt herself tumbling down concrete steps as a skateboarder flew over her, then landing just before another crashed into her head. She saw spatters of her own blood and in that blood the reflection of Ramo-Tep.

"Are they still there?"

Jinx looked back to a young girl, no more than sixteen, crouching on top of some loose tyres, skateboard in hands as she spun the wheels one by one and waited for them to be still again. "Olivia, you know where they at?"

"Last I heard, Lithium Valley," the girl replied. "But they been moving a lot lately on account of all the trouble they been causing. They ambushed some dumb bitch and her crew a while back, stole their turf."

"I know," the Phenyl Barbiedoll said quietly.

"But that's the way of this particular jungle, right?" Jinx said.

"Right. Look, can I ask you a favour?"

Jinx looked her up and down once, smiled. "For you? Sure.

SIX

"Stop staring at my breasts," she said some time later, when the Chevy was parked amongst walls of half-burned tyres that formed part of an elaborate, but unfinished, maze near the upper-west side. "I wish I'd never fucking agreed to this. How the hell am I meant to run in these goddamned things?"

She kicked at the accelerator with one heeled foot and angrily flipped through more pages of the file she had managed to convince Whaley to give her.

"He said he'd organise for the pirate broadcasters to begin immediately – anything yet?"

The Digital Cripple shook his head. "Nothing yet. But .. I'm still a little fuzzy. Anyway I know you said you wanted to get started on this as soon as possible but don't you think we should wait until we have at least *some* new crew to …?"

The Phenyl Barbiedoll silenced him with a raised finger then nodded to where they had driven in. A group of six teenagers, half and half boys and girls, strutted towards them, each wearing a backpack or carrying a holdall. "Here they come."

One of the group raised his goateed chin to them by way of a greeting, pulling back his hood and peeling off his sunglasses. "Whaley," he said.

The Phenyl Barbiedoll nodded. "You must be Jinx."

"Guess so. You got any preferences or you just want us to get to work? Whaley said you want as big a spread as we can manage."

"Uh huh." She stepped out of the car, not used to looking up

He looked at his new mistress, the Phenyl Barbiedoll, and smiled approvingly.

Her hair had been bleached blonde and hung in spirals except for a few finely braided strands near the front. The eye make-up remained as heavy as ever, if applied a little more delicately, but the lipstick had switched from black to bright red. The crop top and combats had gone too, replaced by a full-length sleeveless black cocktail dress with a slit up both sides all the way to her hips that revealed a garter belt on her right thigh. She wore gloves that went up to her elbow of the same black velvet as her dress, rings slipped over them so that each finger sparkled. Combat boots replaced by six-inch heels with straps that were wrapped around her ankle and up her calves. There was a streak of red by one nostril simulating a cocaine haemorrhage and above her breasts a scarification in the shape of chemical strands.

"The Phenyl Barbiedoll," Remy said, just to hear it out loud.

"I feel as fucking moronic as you look, now get in."

FIVE

They had replaced the pick-up truck with a low-riding Chevy which the Phenyl Barbiedoll sat in, arm over the side. The paintwork was once cherry red but was now almost entirely scratched away or covered up by patches repairing rusted holes in the body.

She had parked it at the edge of the wasteland that spread out towards the horizon and where the remnants of the other buildings that had once littered the district lay like corpses. Clouds of smoke from the funeral pyres of diseased animals drifted across the skyline.

She was still on neutral ground, though only just. The other gang members kept their distance, prepared to bide their time. She hadn't seen any of the Felidae just yet but the word would have spread quickly that she was back. She watched as a figure emerged from the lobby, hobbling along on two metal poles that hissed pneumatically as he moved. He looked like a stick insect as he emerged from the shadow of the building.

Whaley had said Remy was now to be known as the Digital Cripple.

"Miss," he said as he stood by the Chevy. She saw now that the crutches were attached permanently to his arms via a series of pins through his elbow and lower arm, effectively extending the limbs to ground level. His legs dangled loosely from his waist, feet slumped on the ground at angles they shouldn't have been able to. The metal plate was now more clearly revealed than ever on a freshly-shaven head, an intricate tattoo encircling it, crawling over his crown and down the back of his neck. Tiny LCD readouts on his metal parts beeped numbers and pulses in a green glow.

FOUR

So then came the shuffling from room to room, floor to floor, past others being painted and pierced and cosmetically enhanced, tailored and trimmed and cut open. For several hours she was subjected to sprays and injections and pipes inserted into every orifice and then came the woman pressing fabrics against her naked body, wrapping things around her thighs and testing them against her breasts to see if the nipple showed through or not. Heads shaking and nodding, arms crossed or flapping around. Make-up applied then removed, re-applied. Hair styled and moussed and waxed and clipped and washed. And in the background, the sound of machines working, hissing and beeping, clicking. Crackly voices over the Tannoy system and bright fluorescent lights, EMPs to her head and so much more.

And at the end of it, she was back in Whaley's office, led through to the attached room that was lined with mirrors on every wall, the ceiling, the floor. You went on forever in that room.

"May I present to you," Whaley said grandly, hands clasped as he unleashed her image on herself, " the *Phenyl Barbiedoll.*"

"Great. Now, lets get started on you."

"Then I want another one."

"And you will, you will. Honey, you're headed straight for TV, I can feel it. But that'll take time. Meanwhile I really would recommend re-branding."

"We're fine the way we are," the Hi-Fi Queen stated flatly.

Whaley grinned, relaxing more that he was getting into his full routine. He straightened his tie and leaned forward on his elbows. His hands had stopped shaking. "Lady, I know no other way to say this to you other than straight but …"

He looked her up and down, shaking his head. The oil-stained combats, the steel toe-capped boots; the chemically-coloured dreadlocked streaks running through her hair and the lip piercing; the crop top and chipped nail polish; the heavy eye make-up and purple lipstick.

"But what?"

"The *Industrial* thing – it just doesn't work anymore. Steel toe-caps? Oh, please. And those trousers, I mean – you do *have* hips under all that don't you?"

"This isn't what I came here to discuss. I'm fine with our current marketing strategy."

"Industrial is *out*. And IMHO, it should never have been *in* in the first place. Some asshole somewhere obviously thought it would be a good idea but thankfully we are seeing the error of his ways. Honey it's *so* last year it isn't even funny."

"That could be because you assigned it to me last year."

"That's true, very true. But last year is last year and this year is this. So if you want my help then you are going to have to work with me. Now can you do that?"

The Hi-Fi Queen sighed. Regardless of her personal dislike of the man he was the best Image Consultant around. He had contacts in every field that was needed and more importantly he knew how to use them – because it was no longer enough just to be tough or smart to rule the streets … you had to have the right marketing campaign behind you too.

"I can do that," she said, measuring her words carefully. "As long as you're quick."

looking at her.

"Don't know why you bother with pissy little bitches like that lot. And zip up for fuck's sake."

Whaley did as instructed, drawing himself back towards the desk and trying to recover a semblance of dignity. His hands shook as he steepled them beneath his chin. "Been a while," he said.

"I've been away."

"Really? Anywhere nice?"

The Hi-Fi Queen leaned forwards, her broad shoulders arching. "Stop. Fucking. Around. I don't know exactly who is responsible for fucking me over but we both know you have your finger in ever little pie there is so …"

"I don't know what you …"

"*Don't*. This will all be a lot easier and quicker if you just *don't*." Whaley swallowed, nodded. "Now, we have a contract. I wish to see that contract fulfilled."

"Ah. If you check the small print, you'll see that the contract terms are only valid up until either a consensual disbanding or … death."

"Do I look dead?"

Whaley shrugged. "About the same as always".

And before he'd even finished the sentence Whaley's head was rebounding off of his desk, blood flying from his nose as he rocked back into his chair.

When he'd recovered, the Hi-Fi Queen said to him, "So are we in agreement here? Your first marketing strategy obviously didn't work. Everyone is dead except the Primary Slave and I - so what are you going to do about it? I want my crew back."

Whaley knew he was cornered and he knew what the Hi-Fi Queen was capable of. The only thing left to do was what he did best – work his pitch.

"Okay, fine. Here's what I think," he began. "Full re-branding, top to bottom. I've got some ideas here that would be perfect for you. I'll give costume and make-up a call and …"

"No. What I want is my crew back."

"But … they're dead."

they did normally. "Step aside."

And then she leaned back, raised one booted foot, and kicked the door to Whaley's office in.

Whaley jumped in his seat, the pen he was gripping flying out of his hands.

"What the fu...?" And he stopped with only one syllable to go when he saw the oversized form of the Hi-Fi Queen looming in his doorway. "Oh my .. What are you doing here?"

"We have some things to discuss," she said, stalking towards him. He seemed frozen behind the desk, locked into the seat. Remy ducked out from behind her, grinning at the other man.

"Can you ... come back? Say in five minutes?"

The Hi-Fi Queen paused, about to get suddenly very angry, then stopped – smiled. She took another two steps towards the desk and looked down. Whaley nervously regarded her, sweat beads forming on his forehead and rolling onto his pressed suit.

"Come on out now honey," the Hi-Fi Queen said, banging twice on the desk with her fist.

"What do you ...?" Whaley began, then stopped as he was eased back from the desk and a green-haired woman emerged from under the desk. She turned and looked up at the Hi-Fi Queen, her lipstick smeared across her face. The Queen gestured over her shoulder.

"Get out."

The woman quickly scrambled out from under the desk, wiping her mouth as she went.

"So how are the Leeches these days?" the Hi-Fi Queen asked as the woman walked past her. "You know, one of these days your bellies are going to burst with all that semen inside you."

The woman said nothing, pushing past the small crowd that had gathered at the doorway.

The Hi-Fi Queen sat down gracefully in the chair on the other side of the desk as Remy picked up the broken door and laid it in the doorway to block it off as best he could.

"So how are you, Whaley?"

"Damn it, I was just about finished," he murmured without

warehouse district and moved into the endless rows of bomb-ruined tenements. "We'll walk the rest of the way."

And they did, across the rubble and piles of wrecked cars, the uprooted TV cabling that the broadcast pirates tapped into and then through the small network of underground aqueducts that stank of the rotting meat of diseased cows and pigs from the nearby meat factories. The whole way the Hi-Fi Queen was reading the symbols sprayed onto every available surface.

"Can you still receive?"

"Most of the time," Remy replied, touching the piece of metal wedged in his head subconsciously. "It's not the same as it used to be."

The Hi-Fi Queen nodded and then they were there, at the main headquarters of the Chrysalis Institute for Public Image. It still looked exactly the same, the subsidence that had gripped the building making it look like it was melting on one side. The top three floors shared a gaping hole at one end and you could see the office workers inside as they moved around, their hair and clothes played with by the winds that blew stronger up there. The whole thing was singed at the edges and little fires still burned within and around it.

The Hi-Fi Queen led the Primary Slave across the cracked marble flooring that preceded the lobby, striding confidently in full view of the other gang members that were on their way in or out. They were safe there, the Institute was neutral territory, but still Remy stuck close to his Mistress just in case. The shocked looks followed them as she kicked open the main double doors then strode past the receptionist who hurriedly finished the line she was snorting and tried to call out but ended up in a coughing fit as some of the drug caught in her throat.

Into the waiting room where a further assemblage of gang members looked up in surprise and confusion. Whispers ran through some; others cautiously placed a hand on their weapons. A second receptionist jumped in front of the Hi-Fi Queen, meekly trying to stop her, dwarfed by the other woman.

"Do you have an appointment?" she asked.

The Hi-Fi Queen just stared down at her. With eyeliner freshly applied, the Queen's eyes looked even bigger and more intense than

THREE

They stuck to the back roads and smaller, disused alleyways of the city as they made their way to the first port of call, the front of the battered pick-up she drove shovelling liquefying garbage bags and soggy boxes aside. It was too soon to show their faces.

Luminescent tag art flashed past them on the high walls, elaborate insignias of the various gangs that helped reignite more memory cells in the Hi-Fi Queen's head. Everything was quickly coming back to her and although she still didn't fully understand *how* what happened had happened, she could at least recall *what* had happened.

"Ramo-Tep is struggling," Remy said, slowing to a halt and pulling in behind an old skip as a crowd of gang members strode past. They looked like members of the Perforated Gallery but piercings were becoming such a common hook that it was no longer a decent judgement of affiliation. "Already one-third of the territory he stole from us has fallen from his hands."

"So I see."

The Hi-Fi Queen had been in the city long enough to be able to read into the graffiti, beyond the simple identification it made and into the structure of the gangs responsible, their motives, their style. Having Remy and his little talents had always helped but they more often than not merely confirmed existing suspicions. Already she was forming a picture of the territories that had formed and fallen and the wars that had been waging, in the time she had been absent.

"Stop here," she said after a while, once they had left the

lazily.

"But Miss, I've been looking after *you*. All the others – they're gone. It's just me now. And you, Miss."

The Hi-Fi Queen didn't answer. She remained with her back to him, the drops of sweat that were cooling on her skin shining like tiny jewels, as she upturned a plastic baggy of angel dust. The drug sparkled as she let it run through her fingers and inside every grain was a tiny fragment of memory.

"Miss?"

Finally she turned, unconcerned by her state of total undress in front of Remy, the Primary Slave. "They're all gone?"

Remy nodded emphatically, his painfully thin form almost lost in his boiler suit.

"Fine," the Hi-Fi Queen announced, standing proudly upright. "Then we have work to do."

Remy smiled widely as he realised his hard work had finally paid off.

She was back – and now the whole world was going to suffer.

egin our revenge."

"Revenge?" She looked down suddenly as something flashed in
her memory and saw the large, perfectly shaped tattoo that blemished
her skin from her belly to just beneath her left breast. It had been
imprinted upon her upside down so that it only truly took shape when
he looked down at it from above. It was an Ankh. "Ramo-Tep," she
murmured.

"You remember? Yes, Ramo-Tep."

Remy scuttled around her, continuing to pluck the machine-
reins from her as she took in her surroundings, recognising the lab piece
by piece. First the workbenches littered with stained test tubes and
beakers, then the cracked wooden shelves piled high with loose sheets
of paper. And the digital clocks, huddled in one corner like sick dogs or
refugees, the boxes of needles and circuitry that were to be her weapons
in her life of warfare.

The battles. The gangs.

Ramo-Tep.

She hissed as Remy stuck her with a needle in her thigh.
"Concentrated vitamin doses, Miss," he said by way of explanation. "I've
been giving them to you ever since I brought you back here."

Strobing blue light from one of the hijacked signs flickered across
the metal plate that bisected his head where it emerged just above his
forehead.

The Hi-Fi queen swivelled and sat upright, then climbed down
off the operating table. Her muscles felt as if they were plated in lead or
filled with the heavy air that surrounds broadcasting stations. She had
to concentrate to place her long legs correctly so that she might walk,
Remy hurrying after her.

"Miss, do you remember? Do you remember what they did to
you?"

The Hi-Fi Queen ran her hands across the rusted joints of the
chemical clamps, skimmed the surface of beakers with the tip of her
finger to remove the scum that had been forming there. "You've not
been looking after the lab, Remy," she said in that slow, mechanical
manner she had as if she were reading from an autocue that was moving

TWO

In the glowing light of neon signs torn from porno shacks along the city's main strip, the Hi-Fi queen finally opened her mascara-smudged eyes a second after all the little monitors Remy had hooked her up to started beeping, buzzing and humming.

"Miss?"

Blue and green and red crossed her eyes, distortions of triple-x phrases warming her pale skin. She sat up slowly, dragging the strips of wire that had been monitoring her life signs for the past three months with her. She had become a chemical interchange with one set of tubes pumping fluids into her and another set pulling it all back in again. The scars has mostly disappeared but a few remained, shiny and white on her naked skin.

"What happened?"

Her vision slowly came into focus again. "Remy?"

"Oh Miss, it's so good to have you *back*!" the man exclaimed, moving quickly around her as if expecting to see some crack in the reality of her return. "You ... you were gone for *so long*."

The Hi-Fi Queen touched her head where her flowing black hair had been partially shaved away to make room for more of Remy's tubing. "Where ... did I go?"

"Into the Static, consumed by the cosmic worms, who knows, Miss," Remy said, plucking one of the tubes from her. She jumped at the spark of pain but was still too dazed to lash out at him as she might otherwise have done. "What matters is that you're back and we can

ONE

During her first reign, the Hi-Fi Queen unleashed her vicious liquid squalor on all those whom she preyed upon, reducing the city's tribal inhabitants to wet piles of regurgitate. She dragged behind her a motley crew of worshippers in the perfect geometric formation of a computer circuit. The Primary Master kept the Primary Slave wrapped coaxial-tight around his wrists, the Secondary followed suit. IDE and SCSCI drew up at the back of the pack, funnelling the pulse-signals of their CPU, the devious hitman Stereo smoothly sweeping from side to side, his split personality soon to become a split physicality after his own assassination. Everything was perfect and functional until Ramo-Tep and the Felidae overturned her Kingdom.

Then came the second reign ...

Eraserhead Press
205 NE Bryant
Portland, OR 97211

email: publisher@eraserheadpress.com
website: www.eraserheadpress.com

Cover Artist: Marco Romano – http://www.fetishbastard.com
Cover Model: Kyron-5 – http://www.kyronfive.com
Cover Design: Simon Logan

ISBN 0-9729598-7-4

THE
DECADENT RETURN
OF THE HI-FI QUEEN
AND HER EMBRYONIC
REPTILE INFECTION

Simon Logan

ERASERHEAD PRESS

"If my 8-bit cybernetic components ever needed a refit, Doctor Simon Logan's backstreet surgery of narrative pragmatism is where I'd aim my rotting sensors; he constructs from the electromagnetic blister-strands of goldfish-memory circuits utter nightmares of what may be. In his latest short novella, Logan paints an apocalyptic horrorscape straight off the back of an old Sex Pistols album cover psycho-montage – there is the Hi-Fi Queen in all her mechanised-nose-pinned glory gnawed on by Man-Dogs and straddled by Lobotomy Blondes, and I sure do want me one of those hyperventilating Phenyl Barbiedolls. Oh, yeah!…"

- *Hertzan Chimera,*
author of Szmonhfu and United States.

Lightning Source UK Ltd.
Milton Keynes UK
03 March 2011

168587UK00001B/100/A